First Te██ ██████

School
for
Stars

KT-514-415

First Term at L'Etoile

School for Stars

Holly & Kelly Willoughby

Orion
Children's Books

First published in Great Britain in 2013
by Orion Children's Books
a division of the Orion Publishing Group Ltd
Orion House
5 Upper St Martin's Lane
London WC2H 9EA
An Hachette UK Company

5 7 9 10 8 6 4

A catalogue record for this book is
available from the British Library

Printed in Great Britain by Clays Ltd, St Ives plc

ISBN 978 1 4440 0811 1

www.orionbooks.co.uk

For our parents, Lynn and Brian, who gave us the world; our husbands, Daniel and David, who mean the world; and our children, Harry, Belle and Lola, who complete our world.

Contents

Hello Story-seeker,

We are the Willoughby sisters and we have a story to share with you. It's a story about one of the most important things in the whole world – friendship.

Our story begins on the first day of term at L'Etoile, School for Stars, with two of our heroines, twins Molly and Maria Fitzfoster, arriving at their new school, L'Etoile. L'Etoile is an exclusive stage school, and takes girls from age ten through to sixteen. With only twenty pupils in each year group, it is considered the best school in the world for producing superstars and has educated some of the most famous names in the history of music and film. To make sure that every student who attends is determined to achieve their life's dream of becoming a star, the enrolment process is not for the faint-hearted.

So sit tight, get ready for laughter and tears, and enjoy this wonderful journey of friendship. We did!

Love from,
Holly and Kelly Willoughby x

1

New Beginnings

Molly and Maria Fitzfoster could barely breathe for nervous excitement as they clutched each other on the back seat of their dad's old Bentley. As the car bounced along the enormous, sweeping drive, they craned their necks out of the window trying to catch a glimpse of their new school. The September sun streaming through the rows of poplar trees completely blinded them.

'Oh, Eddie, are we nearly there yet?' a very exasperated Maria asked their dad's driver. 'We can't see a thing back here!'

'I know, Miss Maria,' Eddie responded. 'The sun is in the wrong spot and making driving a little bit tricky.

I don't think it can be too much further though.'

'Don't worry, Eddie – Maria just hates not being in control. It's not as if we're going to be late or anything. She factored in enough extra journey time to cater for *anything*,' Molly gently mocked her sister.

Maria checked her watch and threw her sister a sarcastic smile.

You see, Maria was extremely well organised. Molly on the other hand was totally the opposite, but more about the twins later . . .

After hitting a few potholes and dodging some wild rabbits, Eddie veered right as the driveway turned sharply, leaving the sun trailing behind and a crystal-clear view ahead. Molly thought to herself that if the sun had been a theatre spotlight, someone had just hollered 'Curtain up!' There stood the school, in all its splendour, nestled against the backdrop of a luscious hillside.

Both girls gasped. The chalk-white building rose majestically out of the green countryside. L'Etoile was everything they had dreamed of – or at least everything *Molly* had dreamed of. Maria, in all honesty, would have preferred to attend a more academic school, but she knew that she would flourish anywhere, and rather than be separated from Molly, with her dreams of stage and screen, she had gone along with her sister's choice.

After all, Story-seeker, you can make more of any situation, when you have a little bit of genius!

'Wow!' exclaimed Molly. 'Mum was right. Quick, Eddie – don't worry about parking, just drop us. We'll work the rest out for ourselves.'

'Now who's *Little Miss Impatient?*' retorted Maria, with a glint in her eye.

The ever-obliging Eddie, as the girls had heard their father call his faithful driver, did as he was instructed and pulled up alongside the grand double-fronted entrance. Fortunately for Eddie and the girls, they had arrived so early that there weren't too many other families around checking their girls in. Almost before the car had come to a stop, Molly and Maria had leapt out and were staring up at the towering black front door. They were transfixed by the enormous gold star door-knocker glistening in the sunlight. It had the words 'Reach for the Stars' inscribed round the edge.

Maria watched that dreamy look she had come to

know and love spread across Molly's face as she read the inscription.

The gold star knocker seemed to be throwing off its own beam of light, warming and mesmerising everything in its path – and the twins were no exception.

'L'E-twa-le . . .' came a frightfully posh and clipped voice through the dark entrance. 'L . . . apostrophe . . . E-T-O-I-L-E.'

As the voice spelled the name of the school, a tall, painfully thin but nonetheless striking figure emerged from the shadows. Suddenly the warmth from the gold star had been eclipsed by a lady with a face caked in make-up, and Molly didn't know whether to laugh or cry.

'Young ladies – or "L'Etoilettes" as you shall now be known. Welcome to L'Etoile, School for the Performing Arts, where only the most gifted of students are accepted. Which of you can tell me what "L'Etoile" means?'

Molly gulped and shot Maria a glance. It was the *as-the-oldest-sister-by-seven-minutes-and-forty-seven-seconds-you're-in-charge* look.

'"L'Etoile" quite simply means "the star" in French,' Maria said, without even the slightest hint of doubt in her voice.

A smile crossed the lady's face. 'Correct, L'Etoilette. And may I have the pleasure of learning your name so I know more about the little star in the making I am addressing?'

'My name is Maria Fitzfoster – and this is my sister, Molly. What's yours?' asked Maria, semi-innocently.

'But of course you are,' the lady replied knowingly, her smile turning into a sickly grin. 'The Fitzfoster Diamond Dynasty twins. How are your dear parents, Brian and Linda? It goes without saying that we know each other well – mixing in the same circles as we do.' She looked both girls up and down, with some approval, it appeared.

'Molly and Maria, I am your new headmistress, Madame Ruby, and you are to think of me as your queen, your mentor and most of all, your inspiration and aspiration. Everything you achieve here at the school, my L'Etoilettes, will set you on the path to superstardom. I, and only I, can make your dreams come true, so let this be the start of something fabulous for us all . . .'

And with that she swooshed round on her stiletto heels and disappeared into the shadows.

'Well!' exclaimed Molly.

'It's OK, Molly,' Maria said, sensing that her sister was still reeling from the make-up.

'My goodness, Maria – did you see her face? How much make-up can one face take?'

'I know – she's a walking blusher brush – but an important one!' said Maria and both girls exploded into a fit of giggles.

Thud . . . thud . . . crash . . . bang . . . wallop!

'What on earth . . .?'

The twins swung round to see the ever-obliging Eddie struggling to drag their matching, designer luggage from the car boot, and immediately ran over to give him a hand. By now more and more cars were beginning to pull up and the chatter and general noise of fearful children and clucking parents swirled about.

Staff members had started to emerge from the main house, equipped with clip-boards stuffed with lists; new student attendance lists; dormitory share lists; dietary requirement lists. In the thirty or so minutes since the Fitzfoster twins had arrived, chaos had engulfed L'Etoile.

Unsure of who they were supposed to register with, Molly decided she'd had enough of headmistresses for one afternoon and opted for the prettiest teacher on the drive – who happened to be the very lovely Miss Helen Hart.

Miss Hart had been teaching at L'Etoile for seven years. She and her family had always had very close links with the school and her father, a man with green fingers, managed its grounds and lovely gardens. Now in her mid-thirties, Helen Hart was a woman of amazing musical talent and had chosen to use her accomplishments to inspire the next generation of potential superstars. When Helen was younger, she'd narrowly missed out on her dream of becoming a world-famous singer/songwriter, having sacrificed her career to look after someone who was ill.

It is from that fact alone, Story-seeker, that you can tell the kind, selfless character of the lovely Miss Hart.

This was her first year as deputy headmistress at L'Etoile – a position she was determined would really make a difference to the students.

'Come on, Maria!' Molly grabbed her sister by the arm and, together, they hurtled towards Miss Hart who was trying to give dorm directions to three chattering girls, who were all asking questions at once.

'One at a time ladies, please . . .' she had a soft lyrical

voice. 'It's important that you take this in as there are two houses at L'Etoile and you need to follow instructions for where to go.'

'Autumn Costello – you are in Monroe House. Follow the yellow flags down past the lake to the West Wing and take this certificate confirming registration to your new housemistress, Mrs Sophie Bell. She'll take it from there.'

'Thank you, Miss Hart,' said Autumn, pretty much courtseying as she backed away towards her parents.

'Actually, Autumn . . .' Miss Hart called after her as she looked down her list. 'Would you mind taking Betsy Harris with you to Monroe – you'll be able to keep each other company. Betsy's majoring in piano too so you'll have plenty to talk about.'

'Absolutely,' said Autumn, trotting back to collect Betsy. 'Hello Betsy – soooo good to meet you. Let's get there early and see if we can share a room, shall we? Come on.' And off they skipped, following the yellow flag road to Monroe.

When Miss Hart had called Autumn back to meet her new companion, the twins had been struck by how young and petrified Betsy had looked. 'She must be quite some pianist!' whispered Maria to Molly, none too quietly. 'She looks about seven!'

'For goodness sake, Maria – when are you going to learn never to judge a book by its cover? Don't you remember that timid little nanny Daddy hired to look after us last summer? You said the same thing about her and look where that got us. She soon found her strength, didn't she?' Molly reminded her sister.

Maria rolled her eyes. Molly always looked for the best in everyone and everything. For twin sisters they really were like chalk and cheese. It's not that Maria was mean, she was just a bit more suspicious of everyone and everything. But that's exactly what balanced the two sisters. Molly's soft, faithful side tempered Maria's cynical outlook – and they loved each other dearly.

The twins hardly noticed the time whizzing by. All around them was a mass of teachers, girls and parents pointing in different directions and talking over each other, not to mention the piles of luggage strewn everywhere. If just one of those bags ended up where it was supposed to be by the end of the day it would be a miracle!

'Now, who's next? asked Miss Hart, looking at the twins.

'Maria and Molly Fitzfoster,' they answered in unison. 'I'm Molly,' said the blonde, 'and I'm Maria,' said the brunette.

Miss Hart stared in earnest at the two faces in front of her, assessing the differences. It was quite amazing. They had the same faces but with completely different colouring. Molly had blue eyes, long blonde wavy hair and an olive hue to her complexion, while Maria had green eyes, long dark wavy hair and a pale, china-doll complexion.

'My goodness, so alike, yet so very different. Would we class you as identical or non-identical twins?' she asked, intrigued.

'That's always been a bit of a conundrum.' Maria took the lead. 'Officially, we're identical twins, but physically now we don't look much alike.'

'Dad calls us Snow White and Rose Red because we remind him of that fairy tale,' Molly piped up. It was so typical of her to get all romantic at a time like this, thought Maria.

'Well, here at L'Etoile, you are all individuals,' continued Miss Hart. 'You've come to this school to be yourselves and find yourselves and you are both very welcome – as starlets in the making. Now let's see which houses you're in . . .' She flipped through the lists on her bulging clipboard.

The twins gulped and shot each other a look of panic. Houses . . . plural . . . not one house together?

Even with all this talk about individuality and finding themselves, neither was ready to be without the other just yet!

'Ah yes, here we are . . . Molly, you're in Garland House.' Molly's eyes started to prickle with tears. 'And Maria, let's see now . . . won't that be nice for you both – you're in Garland House too.'

The relief! Maria flung her arm around her sister's shoulder and grabbed the two registration certificates Miss Hart was holding out for them.

'Garland House is a separate building behind the main school towards the theatre. It's a grand white building with pillars at the entrance. Follow the blue flags along the path. Your new housemistress, Miss Mary Coates, will meet you in the entrance hall and show you to your room. Good luck, girls, and be sure to work hard.'

Molly and Maria nodded, again in unison, and bounded over to the ever-obliging Eddie, twittering about Garland House. 'Come on, Eddie! I'm desperate to see our new room and to meet the other girls!'

Eddie lolloped after them dragging two huge suitcases while the girls pranced in front trailing their coats, certificates and school bags.

'Watch out, Molly!' shrieked Maria, leaping on her

sister just in time, knocking them both backwards over a low hedge onto the lawn.

At that very moment, an enormous, sleek, black car came careering round the turning circle and screeched to a halt halfway across the lavender-lined footpath the twins had been walking along.

There was a stunned silence as everyone who was still on the gravel watched as the car doors were flung open and three rather hideous but extremely famous faces stepped out (and one rather pudgy face who no one recognised). Molly and Maria were still catching their breath and Eddie scrabbling for strewn clothing when they heard an American accent say, 'Oh for heaven's sake, Blue, darling, I told you not to drive yourself any more . . . that's why we have chauffeurs. You never were much good at knowing when to stop.' There was a muffled gasp as the very beautiful Mrs Serafina Marciano stood straightening her very expensive haute-couture suit.

'Lucinda honey, ignore your mommy,' a baritone American voice drawled back. 'Go find out where we need to drop your stuff so I can get outta here. I've got a meeting with Universal Pictures in London Town in an hour and I'm already running crazy late.'

'Pop, Mommy, I already know which house we're

in. Mommy requested Garland House when she spoke with Madame Ruby in the summer. It's where all the big stars graduate from.' Then Lucinda turned to her mother and said in the snobbiest tone she could muster, 'We should sooo have come in the private Garland entrance to avoid the *others*.'

'Darling, remember what I told you. It's all about making an entrance. What you do with that entrance is up to you.' And Mrs Marciano replaced her Hollywood-dark sunglasses back on the immaculately powdered bridge of her cosmetically altered little nose.

And there begins the nightmare, Story-seeker, with the arrival of Lucinda Marciano, daughter to Hollywood's very own royalty, Blue and Serafina Marciano.

Every single person recognised them from numerous Hollywood blockbuster movies and red-carpet events, which Blue directed and Serafina starred in. Most recently they'd filmed a documentary from their home in Los Angeles called *At Home With The Marcianos*, where the whole world had got to know the family – including the young Lucinda in all her horrendous glory.

Even the Fitzfosters had tuned in to watch it. Molly had been shocked to see how unhappy and obnoxious Lucinda Marciano had appeared on the show. It was evident that she had everything she could possibly wish for, just like the Fitzfosters, yet Molly and Maria weren't spoiled and mean like Lucinda. Their mum had explained that it was unfair to blame Lucinda. She said the fault lay with the lack of time and effort that the Marcianos invested in their daughter. She was an only child so had no brothers or sisters to turn to and her parents evidently had little or no time in their busy schedules to guide and discipline her. Mrs Fitzfoster went on to explain how Molly and Maria had always had each other to lean on and that she and their father made sure they knew the value of having everything and nothing in equal measure.

Maria, having dusted herself down, was fuming at the Marcianos' blatant disregard for the rest of the human race and was marching up to Lucinda, one arm gesticulating in anger as she got ready to tell her exactly what she thought about her *big entrance*. But before she had time to even open her mouth, Lucinda promptly threw her coat over Maria's outstretched arm.

'Oh thank goodness. There are staff!' Lucinda snapped. 'Take that to my room, will you?' And she turned her back on Maria, whose jaw had hit the floor in shock.

(And it is not very often that our Maria is speechless, Story-seeker.)

Maria silently counted to ten, threw the coat on the ground and strode back to Molly and Eddie, her eyes wide with fury as she plotted exactly what to do with her anger. She vowed to dedicate herself to upholding the student balance and to never let Lucinda – or Lucifette as she would now be known – tip the scales of the entire school in her favour. Maybe the way she behaved wasn't all her fault but, even so, Maria wasn't going to let her get away with that sort of performance.

'Who's in charge around here?' stormed Blue Marciano, glaring at every single member of staff in turn.

Helen Hart suddenly realised that in her new capacity as Deputy Head, she out-ranked everyone else on the gravel.

'Mr Marciano . . .' she ventured. 'Welcome to L'Etoile, School for . . .' but she was rudely interrupted.

'FOR STARS . . .' There it was again, the clipped voice from the shadows that had greeted the twins when they'd arrived.

'Dearest Mr Marciano, Mrs Marciano . . . I am Madame Ruby, Headmistress – we spoke on the phone in June.' She held out an immaculately manicured hand for Blue to shake (or kiss!). 'Please, do follow me. You are, of course, our most esteemed guests and I would like to escort you and your lovely daughter personally to Garland House. We have held our very best room for Lucinda and her L'Etoile companion.'

With that all eyes swivelled to the fourth person to emerge from the car – the one nobody had recognised. Madame Ruby beckoned to her, but could hardly hide her surprise as the slightly plump, awkward girl approached.

'And you are?' she enquired in an intimidating tone.

'S . . . S . . . S . . . Sally Sudbury, Madame,' the girl stammered.

'Sally Sidekick more like,' whispered Maria to Eddie and Molly, who grinned in agreement.

For the audience on the driveway, the whole scene

was as ridiculous as it was spectacular and heads bobbed from one direction of conversation to the other, as though they were watching a mixed doubles final at Wimbledon.

'Welcome, Miss Sudbury, to our school of excellence.'

Sally shrank at the mention of the word 'excellence'. She'd never been particularly excellent at anything. Sally was the daughter of Maggie Sudbury, the Marcianos' housekeeper. Maggie had come to work for the family as a struggling, single mother, with baby Sally, who the family were kind enough to accommodate as part of her domestic arrangement. As the years went by, Sally had become a sort of playmate for Lucinda. Now she was burdened with the role of 'companion' and had spent her entire life in Lucinda's shadow. Blinded by the privileged life that she thought Sally was experiencing alongside Lucinda, Maggie was unable to see the damage that this was doing.

'Erm, thank you, Madame . . .' she mumbled. But no sooner had she finished speaking than Lucinda yanked her by the arm.

'Move it, Sally – since when did this become about you? You've got my unpacking to do!'

And with that, the whole Marciano clan, plus

poor Sally, were marched off through the main L'Etoile entrance by Madame Ruby, brushing past the gold star knocker as they went, obviously getting a private tour before being shown to the 'best' Garland accommodation.

Only Maria, who had regained her calm, broke the stunned silence. 'Come on, Molly . . . let's check out our room – I'm sure it's just as fabulous. Who does that little Lucifette think she is? She'll keep – she'd best hope we don't run into each other too often!'

But you know, and I know, Story-seeker, that that would be just too easy!

2

And Then There Were Three

'I know we haven't seen Monroe House yet, but isn't Garland beautiful?' exclaimed Molly dreamily as she sat at her new dressing-table brushing her long, blonde hair.

The girls counted themselves very lucky so far. Their new housemistress, Miss Coates, had greeted them in the entrance hall and had been really sweet – a real 'mummy' type who Molly had instantly felt she could turn to if she was homesick – and who Maria knew she could run rings around! The only thing they hadn't foreseen was that there was a third bed in their room.

'Who do you think we'll get?' asked Molly thoughtfully.

'Whoever it is, she'll be hard pushed to beat Lucifette in the annoying stakes, so I'll take my chances. Anyway, you love a project, Moll – I'm sure you'll be able to dress her up and do her hair just how you'd love to still do mine!' Maria answered triumphantly from under the bed.

'Maria – what are you doing under there?' asked Molly, chuckling at how her sister still had the price tags stuck to the bottom of her shoes. Some people have no idea, she thought quietly to herself.

'Huh?' Maria wriggled out onto the bedroom floor, looking as if she'd been dragged through a hedge backwards. 'I wish I'd spotted how few plug sockets there were before Eddie left. How am I going to run a business from here? I'll have to email Dad and ask him to post me a multi-socket tonight.' She began picking balls of dust and who knows what else from her cardigan.

'You are funny, the way you talk. You're hardly running a business . . . it's more of a hobby,' Molly said, looking in disbelief at Maria's cardigan. How could she get so messy, so quickly?

'But,' said Maria, ignoring Molly's look, 'someone's got a responsibility to dig out the truth and keep the rest of the school informed, haven't they? I think that running an online blog here under the radar is a great idea – and as far as I'm concerned it *is* a business – everyone's business is my business – so, ha!' And they both laughed.

Maria's life-long dream was to become one of the world's hottest, finger-on-the-pulse journalists, and in her eyes she wasn't too young to start gaining some work experience. At the beginning of the summer holidays, she'd convinced her dad to set her up with a basic website that she could update by herself. She'd sold the idea to him as an *online community website* to keep their village up-to-date with what was going on.

Her dad – perhaps somewhat naïve about his daughter – had considered it a good way for her to learn about people in her community and keep them abreast of village events such as the Summer Fête, the St Mary's Charity Fun Run, and to help promote local businesses by raising awareness of their services. That summer Maria had made sure she accompanied her mum to various village meetings and experimented with her talents by interviewing community members, such as the farmer during lambing season, the butcher about his award-winning pear-and-pork sausages, the florist working on a local celebrity wedding, to name but a few. She wrote articles about her findings, with a little bit of community gossip thrown in for good measure, and by the time she left Little Hampton, she had managed to acquire quite a name for herself.

Her village website had been called *See it Like Maria*, but now that she no longer considered herself an amateur blogger, and was about to enter a new school community, she decided it would be much more fun to run an anonymous blog called 'Yours, L'Etoilette' – a report written by a mystery student, for the students. She'd have to spread the word about the site somehow – under the radar, of course, to avoid unwanted teacher attention – so that the girls would know where to go to get their fix of genuinely useful info about school events but (more importantly) a good bit of gossip as well. An additional feature she'd been toying with was to find a way for students to contact the mysterious 'Yours, L'Etoilette' with their comments or needs so the site could have an agony-aunt element to it, or an 'advertise for help' service. But she'd have the whole term to perfect that.

To put it bluntly, Story-seeker, Maria was more excited about this little project than any musical feats she might achieve at L'Etoile!

While Maria busied herself setting up her 'home office', Molly unpacked for both of them, filling every available drawer with clothes and toiletries and laying out their new school uniforms ready for the first day of term tomorrow.

'What do you think of these school skirts, Mimi?' she asked, using her favourite pet name for Maria.

'A skirt's a skirt, isn't it?' answered Maria, who was busy untangling about a thousand charger wires from Molly's hairdryer. She'd labelled them all clearly but couldn't account for Molly's erratic 'stuffing into a bag' method of packing.

'Are you kidding? Look how long these skirts are. Do you think we'll get away with rolling them up a bit? These are soooooo long and gross!' Molly said in despair, already dreaming up ten different ways she could make these blue and grey uniforms look cool. The girls had worn what they liked at their junior school, so this was a new experience for both of them. Molly was even more fashion-conscious than she was beauty-conscious – if that was possible – and it was fair to say that she had a natural flair for what was hot and what was definitely not!

'Oh well – at least I won't have to hold you up in the mornings now deciding what to wear,' said Molly, half-regretfully, as she stared down at the grey pleated skirt, grey tights, pale blue-and-white check shirt and navy blue V-neck jumper.

There was a knock on the bedroom door and Miss Coates appeared.

'Molly . . . Maria . . .' She looked from left to right, commanding the girls' attention. 'I'd like you to meet your new roommate for the year, Pippa Burrows.'

Pippa peered at them from behind Miss Coates and smiled shyly at the girls.

'Hi,' she whispered.

Molly jumped up from her suitcase which, despite her best efforts, still looked as if it had just thrown up on the floor by her bed. 'Hello Pippa. Really pleased to meet you. This is my sister Maria. We've been wondering who might be sharing with us. We're so happy it's you.'

Maria stifled the desire to roll her eyes at Molly's immediate tendency to *love* at first sight and managed a genuine smile of acceptance. Pointing over to the bed under the window she said, 'Molly and I left you the nicest bed as we already know each other, obviously, and don't mind being quite close together.'

It wasn't a huge bedroom so Miss Coates was

delighted to see that the twins had been generous and thoughtful to their new roommate.

'Thank you very much,' said Pippa and started dragging her beaten-up old suitcase over to her bed.

'We'll help you,' said Molly. 'Probably best if we put it straight on the bed. We've got ourselves in a bit of a mess already in here.'

'OK, girls. I'll leave you three to get to know each other. It's a picnic supper of jam sandwiches in your rooms tonight while you settle in.' And Miss Coates handed Molly a large paper bag filled with squidgy packages. 'Bedtime is at eight o'clock sharp. You'll all be exhausted after the excitement of this afternoon and ready for a good night's sleep. You'll hear the bell chime five minutes before lights out. I'm in the room at the end of the corridor if you need anything. My name is on the door.' And with that she left the girls alone, clicking the door shut behind her.

Molly, Maria and Pippa stood and looked at each other for a moment. They could hear other students in their rooms laughing and shouting at the top of their voices; things like, 'Has anyone got a spare toothbrush?' and 'Oh no, I've forgotten my school tights. Does anyone have a spare pair?'

Maria was the first to break the awkward silence.

'Molly, if you even think about rushing down the corridor with our toothbrushes so we have to use our fingers – or share poor Pippa's – I'll kill you!'

Without hesitation, Pippa shot Maria a look of understanding and dived on her suitcase as if to protect her toiletries and underwear with her life. After unpacking, all three girls joked and shared sandwiches until lights out.

So there you have it, Story-seeker. If only they knew on that first night that they would become the three corners of a triangle of friendship which would last for a lifetime.

★ ★ ★

3

Learning the Ropes

The school bell rang at the end of the first day at L'Etoile. And what a day it had been. All the first-years had been running around the school like headless chickens working out the quickest route to this class and that.

The twins had quickly realised that Lucinda had been right about one thing – there were loads of really talented people in Garland House. It was easy to tell one house student from another as the Monroe L'Etoilettes were in the exact same grey skirts and tights but wore yellow check shirts and V-neck jumpers. Molly, needless to say, was delighted when it dawned on her in assembly that morning how close her blonde locks had actually come to clashing with a luminous canary-coloured sweater.

Assembly had been held in the school theatre – aptly named the 'Kodak Hall' for obvious Oscar reasons. Indeed, the school had ridiculously over-inflated, celebrity-league names for most of its rooms. The music rooms were called the 'Royal Albert Rooms'; the sports hall was called the 'Athenae Olympic Quadrant'; the science and maths block, the 'Einstein Quarter'; the dance studio the 'Bolshoi Suite'; the English and foreign language rooms the 'Shakespeare and Latin Quarter' – the dining room was even called the 'Ivy Room', for goodness sake. Maria's eye-rolling was even beginning to get on her own nerves, but Molly and Pippa were in awe of everything – appreciating every not-so-subtle reference to the great and good. Maria took pleasure, though, in seeing her sister happy and, to be perfectly honest, their new-found friend Pippa as well. At least with her there, she didn't have to join in with Molly's every dreamy whim. Thank goodness for Pippa Burrows.

The whole school, approximately a hundred students at any one time, had all filed into the hall, split according to Garland and Monroe houses. Madame Ruby was joined on the stage by all the teachers. For Maria – who was desperately trying to remember every single face to write her first blog of the year – it was the perfect line-up to start off the proceedings.

Miss Hart sat to Madame Ruby's right – although set slightly back so as not to be seen to be 'on the same level' as Madame.

The girls' Garland housemistress, Miss Coates, and Mrs Bell, the housemistress for Monroe, sat to her left. The other teachers sat in rows behind. Beyond their striking appearance as a somewhat eccentric collection, they remained a bit of a mystery to the first-year students. Maria had made a mental note to start filtering through past years' student magazines to check what the teachers were really like.

'My L'Etoilettes,' Madame Ruby addressed her audience, 'On this, the first day of the new school year, there are those among you for whom this is the beginning of the rest of your star-seeking lives, and there are those who are already in that star-seeking process, but you have one crucial thing in common. You are in the world's very best establishment to mould your careers as superstars.' She drew a short breath.

'May I share with you a piece of advice passed on to me as a starlet by my great grandmother and founder of L'Etoile, the great Lola Rose D'Arcy . . . Be true to yourselves and your talent and in doing so you will achieve your potential. Reach for the stars, L'Etoilettes, reach for the stars!'

A round of applause erupted. Only Maria sat manically scribbling away on the notepad she'd smuggled in between the band of her rolled-up skirt and her hideous grey tights.

'From this moment on,' Madame Ruby continued, 'we, the loyal, talented teaching staff at L'Etoile, promise to guide and develop your individual artistic talents to their utmost potential. And in return we ask that you are receptive to every criticism and note. So go forth, L'Etoilettes, and become the stars your namesake school can be proud of for years to come.'

Another enraptured round of applause followed. For all the dodgy make-up, even Maria couldn't deny the excitement and zeal Madame Ruby made her pupils feel.

After assembly, the girls made their way to the classroom numbers they had been given that morning by their housemistresses.

Thankfully, Molly, Maria and Pippa had once again been banded together in Form 1 Alpha under the tutelage of the slightly alarmingly named Mrs Rene Spittleforth.

Mrs Spittleforth had horn-rimmed spectacles and

was wearing what could only be described as a violet and daffodil print tabard! She was, to all intents and purposes, a very nice lady – the girls thought she was about forty years old – but then, to them, anyone over twenty-one seemed about forty years old.

Their first hour in the classroom began with Miss Spittleforth standing in front of a large whiteboard, explaining their timetable.

A school day at L'Etoile was divided into two sections. Morning classes were sciences, languages, history and geography. Then each afternoon would focus on the special L'Etoile arts of music, dance and drama. During the enrolment process, every student had had to demonstrate a particular skill to an exceedingly high level before they could be awarded one of the 'gold-dust' places at the school. These skills could take the form of being a budding concert musician, an exquisite classical or modern dancer, a talented actress of stage and screen or an incredible vocalist. Or, like Lucinda, you had to have a face that fitted and parents with bulging bank accounts and friends in high places who could benefit the school's standing.

Next there was class registration – students had to report to their assigned class tutors at nine o'clock every morning. Each member of the class was given a number between one and ten, according to where their names fell alphabetically, to call out as proof that they were in the room. Maria had thought how easy it would be for Molly to answer twice while she was up to mischief elsewhere.

Molly and Maria were numbers four and five. Just for that morning's registration, every girl was asked to stand up when they called their number, and give their name and their artistic talent by way of an introduction to their fellow pupils.

Form 1 Alpha was a mixture of Garland and Monroe students:

♪ Form 1 Alpha ♪

Lydia Ambrose	Monroe Cellist & Double Bassist
Belle Brown	Garland Classical Ballet Dancer
Pippa Burrows	Garland Singer/Songwriter
Maria Fitzfoster	Garland Pianist
Molly Fitzfoster	Garland Singer & Actress
Amanda Lloyd	Garland Dancer
Daisy Mansfield	Monroe Bassoonist
Alice Parry	Garland Singer & Actress
Sofia Vincenzi	Monroe Singer & Actress
Lara Walters	Monroe Drummer & Percussionist

Believe us when we tell you, Story-seeker,
that you should make a note of these names –
for most, if not all of them, will walk the halls
of fame for generations to come.

It is true to say that Molly had the voice of an angel and a delicate subtlety as an actress, which one is born with rather than taught. Maria, in her expert knowledge of, well everything, recognised and appreciated that L'Etoile was the only place in the world that could harness and nurture her sister's natural ability, which is why she hadn't put up much of a fight when it was decided the girls would both apply to be L'Etoilettes. Maria's musical speciality was playing the piano. She was, of course, as much of a genius at that as at everything else she did. No one could argue that she had been given a place because of the social standing of her family. She really was a very clever girl.

As luck would have it for the whole of 1 Alpha, Lucinda and Sally Sudbury were in the other class, 1 Beta, with eight other girls who would no doubt be endlessly tormented by Lucinda's taunts and boring chatter. Their class registration session ran as follows:

♪ Form 1 Beta ♪

Nancy Althorpe	Monroe Actress
Autumn Costello	Monroe Pianist
Betsy Harris	Monroe Pianist
Elizabeth Jinks	Monroe Dancer
Charlotte Kissimee	Monroe Singer
Lucinda Marciano	Garland Singer & Actress
Corine Sequoia	Garland Singer & Actress
Heavenly Smith	Garland Dancer
Sally Sudbury	Garland Actress
Faye Summers	Garland Fashion Student

And so it was that our three heroines had so far that day magnificently managed to avoid any direct contact with the undesirable Lucinda Marciano. Pippa had narrowly avoided a situation earlier that evening when she had nearly bumped trays with Lucinda in the Ivy Room during the mad scramble for dinner. Luckily for her on this occasion, the rotund, red-faced, head dinner lady, Mrs Mackle, chose that exact moment to haul a mortified Sally Sudbury out of the dinner queue directly in front of their collision after observing her queuing up for seconds. This distraction gave Pippa just enough time to bomb over to the opposite side of the dining room to the safety of the Fitzfoster twins before Lucinda noticed. Thank goodness for small mercies and busybody cooks!

4

Midnight Feasts and Girly Chats

*T*hat night after lights out, Molly, Maria and Pippa had decided on a torchlight *not-so-midnight-more-like-nine-o'clock-but-who-cares* feast to mull over the day's events.

'So, Pippa . . .' Molly said, as the three girls lay snuggled up in their beds munching on fondant fancies.

'Hold on . . .' Maria interrupted. 'I can't see a bloomin' thing in this tuck box Mum packed, and my torch doesn't seem to want to work with or without batteries!'

Pippa reached an arm from the warmth of her duvet, leaned over to the window and yanked the curtain back to allow a little moonlight into the room.

Maria looked up, impressed at Pippa's solution, and Molly continued, delighted not to have been delayed for another ten minutes, while her ever-efficient sister worked her way through an entire battery pack.

'Tell us about you, Pippa. It suddenly dawned on me while I was brushing my teeth tonight that I don't know anything about you really – other than you're pretty cool!'

'What do you want to know?' Pippa asked through a mouthful of pink sponge cake.

'You know – where you grew up, what your mum and dad are like, whether you have any brothers or sisters, where you went to school – that kind of thing,' said Molly.

Pippa took a deep breath. This had been her biggest fear before coming to L'Etoile. She was confident enough in her talents as a singer/songwriter, but she thought her rather impoverished family roots might prevent her from fitting in with the more privileged girls. And here she was, having a mid-evening feast with two of the most glamorous students in her year, and being asked to talk about herself.

'I'm on a scholarship,' she blurted out. Molly looked blankly at Maria, who was nodding warmly in Pippa's direction, willing her to go on.

'A scholarship, Molly,' Pippa continued, 'is for students whose families can't necessarily afford to send them to an incredible school like this because it costs too much money. But rather than both the school and the student missing out on each other – for, as we all know, both benefit from talent – the school sometimes offers one or two places a year free of charge to someone who deserves a chance. That's what happened to me and my family – or I should say to me and Mum – there's just the two of us at home.'

'Where's home?' asked Molly, absent-mindedly, as she struggled to extract a boiled sweet which had stuck to its own wrapper.

'Oh, do put a sweet in it, Moll,' shushed Maria. 'Let the girl speak, for heaven's sake. You've already asked enough questions!'

Molly, realising her insensitivity, sat back and put both the sweet and the wrapper into her mouth.

'Home,' continued Pippa, 'is near Clapham Junction in London. Mum's a special needs teacher by day in a local school, and a legal secretary by night. She's always worked long hours to try and bring in as much money as she can for us without losing out on doing what she really loves, which is working with the children who need her most.'

Molly could feel tears in her eyes – thank goodness it was dark.

At that point, Maria jumped in. 'Well, to be honest, Pips – that's not entirely unlike us. We just had a few more people around. Dad runs the family diamond business and works all the hours under the sun – in fact we only really see him on holiday, and Mum, although she's around all the time, spends hours on local charity and council work. Sounds like we all come from really kind families though, which is why we probably get on like we do.'

Bless her, thought Pippa, bemused but touched. You couldn't get two more different families; but she loved Maria for trying to put her at ease.

'When you put it like that, I suppose you're right. I hadn't thought of it that way,' she said.

Maria was on a roll. 'Look at it another way, there's a glaringly obvious case of it's not WHAT you have that makes you a good person, it's WHO you have around you in life. That awful Lucifette comes from money like Molly and me but the difference is that no one around her cares about anything other than money and fame. That's what makes her such an insensitive, self-absorbed little witch.'

'All right, Maria, we get your point,' Molly said.

'Carry on, Pippa. How did you come to apply for L'Etoile then? Have you always wanted to be a singer? Can't wait to hear you sing, PS!'

Pippa laughed. Molly's little Mollyisms were so adorable. She abbreviated everything where she could get away with it: BTW – by the way . . . FYI – for your information . . . FGS – for goodness sake . . . and they were just the few she'd used today.

'Well . . .' continued Pippa, 'or should I say FYI, Miss Molly? L'Etoile actually approached me!'

'What?' The twins sat bolt upright in tandem, Maria knocking a bag of cola bottles all over the floor as she did so.

'I know!' exclaimed Pippa. 'It was completely crazy. I'd just got in from school on the day we broke up for the summer and the phone was ringing. Mum was still at work so I answered it and you'll never guess who was phoning.'

'Not the Grand Madame herself?' Molly gasped, wide-eyed and incredulous.

'Not quite,' answered Pippa. 'But second best. It was Miss Hart, the deputy head. She's really nice, by the way.'

'I know, BTW,' said Molly who had now hopped onto the end of Pippa's bed and helped herself to some duvet. 'She's the one who first checked us in on the drive yesterday. I picked her as she looked the nicest teacher. So then what happened?'

'Well,' said Pippa, happy to be sharing her story at last, 'Not sure if I told you or not, but I write songs as well as sing. My Uncle Harry has a little studio at the bottom of the garden so I used to spend the weeknights while Mum was at work, writing lyrics and singing into the voice recorder on Mum's computer. Then on a Sunday afternoon, I'd go over to Uncle Harry's and we'd try and lay down onto track what I'd been working on. He always seemed quite excited by what I'd done. I had no real idea – you can't really gauge how good you are yourself, can you?'

'Oh, I don't know,' Maria joked. 'Moll never seems to struggle with that kind of humility!' Molly swiped at Maria's duvet and another bag of sweets emptied itself all over the bedroom floor. 'Ooops,' she said and turned back to Pippa. 'Go on, go on.'

Pippa giggled at them. 'Sorry, where was I?'

'Uncle Harry's shed,' said Maria.

'Yes, Uncle Harry's *studio*,' she said. 'So anyway, after a few months, my Uncle Harry said that there was a website where you could create your own page and upload songs and performances for people to rate, so I did, and next thing I know Miss Hart is on the phone saying that she's heard me singing online, asking me if I really wrote the songs myself and could she make an appointment to come over to meet me and my mum!'

'What, just like that?' Maria asked.

'Just like that,' Pippa finished.

'Wowsers, it's so perfect and romantic. What a way to get discovered. To be recognised for your true talent and potential. It's just fabulous,' said Molly, scooping up a handful of dusty cola bottles from the floor.

'Wait until Lucifette hears your story. It will infuriate her into orbit,' chuckled Maria. At which point the very useless torch on her lap miraculously started throwing out enough light to illuminate a small stadium.

'Maria, turn it off, we'll get totally busted!' Molly scrambled back into her own bed in a panic.

A mixture of full tummies and tales of stardom had tipped the girls over the edge and within seconds of Maria switching off the super-torch, they were fast asleep, dreaming of over-achievement!

5

Mackle the Jackal

*A*fter an endlessly long week of boring mornings and fun afternoons spent doing what each girl loved to do best – perform – Forms 1 Alpha and 1 Beta learned that they were finally going to get together for the weekly Friday Afternoon Entertainment Session. This was an opportunity for each of the twenty students in the first year group to put on a display for her classmates of her favourite achievement of the week. The girls were told during classical ballet (on the first Thursday of term), which immediately sent them into a massive panic at the thought that they had less than twenty-four hours to prepare. Luckily though, the performance was to start the following

Friday so they had plenty of time to discuss and think about what they'd do.

'If I never see or hear that sickly sweet Seminova woman again, it'll be too soon,' Maria groaned, launching her ballet shoes into the bedroom so violently that they landed in a puddle in the sink.

Miss Natalia Seminova had spent most of her life training and performing for the world-famous Bolshoi Ballet in Moscow and most recently in New York. She had the most immaculate credentials of any ballet teacher, and the sweetest nature. She would put the girls through their paces every second Thursday; modern dance, hip-hop, tap and jazz. Miss Seminova had told them that L'Etoile's dance focus was mainly on ballet for discipline and posture. The more fun genres of dance could be added to a L'Etoilette's repetoire with ease at any time.

'Well, I think she's the perfect ballet mistress,' said Molly.

'Me too,' agreed Pippa. 'I've never done ballet before in my life and I was completely dreading it. I mean, be honest, girls – look at me – it's more suited to Maria, and that's saying something!' Maria grimaced. She was not, nor did she ever plan to be, a ballerina!

Pippa did kind of have a point though. She was taller than most of the other girls in her class, with a slender, willowy body, dark eyes framed by luscious black lashes, and long raven-coloured hair which tumbled wildly down her back. She was striking in a way that no amount of styling could create. Her wild-child appearance just needed taming slightly – or perhaps *refining* would be a better word, and then it'd be a case of 'watch out L'Etoilettes – here comes Pippa Burrows!'

Molly, had of course, been desperate to get the straighteners out and untangle those crazy locks. One good thing to come out of Pippa's arrival, though, was that Molly had officially become thankful for school uniforms, after seeing – and in fact successfully enduring, some of the outfits Pippa had in her wardrobe. It had taken some strength of character for Molly to hold back, but her sensitive side won the battle and she temporarily put her thoughts on ice. She needed to feel confident that their friendship was completely cemented before she would tactfully attempt to transform this little wild duckling into the swan she knew Pippa could be.

The happy trio changed out of their ballet things and, half-starving after two hours – or near enough –

of relentless pliés and pirouettes, flitted like gazelles to the Ivy Room for supper.

'Come on, let's eat. I'm sooooo hungry,' pleaded Molly. 'And let's use dinnertime to talk about what on earth we're going to perform at the group session next Friday. Eeeek!'

They were pretty late for dinner, which on the one hand meant no queue, but it also meant that most of the decent food had already been scoffed.

Molly, who was a fussy eater at the best of times, and certainly no fan of L'Etoile school dinners, had been mostly living on a diet of bread and cola bottles the whole week. Maria, on the contrary, was concerned that she was starting to put on a few pounds. Every mealtime she was trying to clear Molly's plate and her own to avoid the wrath of Mackle the Jackal, L'Etoile's infamous dinner lady!

It was poor Betsy Harris who had so brilliantly nicknamed Mackle, because of the way she scavenged through the leftovers, as a jackal would an old carcass. Like Molly, Betsy was also finding mealtimes hard to swallow, but she didn't have a Maria to protect her, and was always left sitting at the table by the exit doors, as an example to everyone, being made to stomach every last morsel. Mackle the Jackal would stand, with one fat elbow resting on the work surface, just at the point where the girls put their trays down on the runners to scrape off the leftovers. Her beady, shark-like eyes darted over every plate that passed under her nose, checking for anyone who'd left too much food.

The twins and Pippa entered the dining room just in time to see Mackle the Jackal's fat hand come down on Betsy's plate for the fourth dinnertime that week – or near enough eighth if you included lunchtimes as well!

'Betsy Harris!' Mackle spat, and as she did so a bit of semi-chewed food escaped from her mouth and sat on her top lip – moving up and down in a disgustingly hypnotising manner every time she spoke.

'Betsy Harris,' she repeated. 'How does it feel, Betsy, to be the most famous student in your year? Hit the giddy heights of fame a little sooner than expected, eh!?!' In her excitement, Mackle had produced a little too much saliva, which thankfully dislodged the piece of rogue food from her lip – but made her look like a drooling, rabid animal hovering over her kill.

'I . . . I . . . I beg your pardon, Mrs Mackle. Famous, you say?' said the terrified Betsy.

'Yesssssss, Harris!' Mackle hissed. 'Yours is the only name everyone hears day in, day out, in this dining room. When are you going to learn to eat up! Those sprouts will put hairs on your chest!'

The whole dining room winced in horror.

'What, and have a hairy chest – and top lip . . . and chin – like her!' Daisy Mansfield the bassoonist stage-whispered to the other Monroe girls behind her in the queue.

'Daiissseee – careful,' hissed Lydia Ambrose (cellist) who was a couple of places behind Daisy in the dinner queue. She'll hear you and then you'll be for it!'

'She won't hear me from all the way down there – she's probably eaten so much of the decent stuff and cooked up all the rubbish that's left for us, her body can't take any more. Did you see her spitting food as she spoke? It's coming out of her mouth, her nose, even her ears!' Daisy continued daringly – delighted to be getting some sniggers from her peers.

'Oh, so that's what they call cauliflower ears!' Maria said – with perfect comedy timing. At which point, the seven girls now left waiting to collect their meals dissolved into muffled, *you-know-you-shouldn't-be-laughing-but-you-just-can't-stop* hysterics.

Betsy's roomate, the pianist Autumn Costello, jumped up from the table where she was struggling to eat her own supper. 'Oh please stop, girls – poor Betsy will think you're laughing at her – or worse, Mackle will think she's the one being humorous and continue the torture. It truly is bullying of the most horrible kind.'

Pippa, who hadn't uttered a single word during the whole horror show, was deep in thought about how to beat the Jackal so that she'd never be able to bully anyone ever, ever again. She'd been subjected to bullying at her junior school and when she'd left those small-minded Jenson brothers behind, she had vowed that she'd never be a victim again and would always help others in need.

'Guys . . . guys . . .' She grabbed Maria and Molly. 'We've got to help her. Any minute now she's going to throw up – and then she'll probably be forced to eat that too!' Molly gagged at the thought.

'Welcome to my world,' said Maria sharply. 'Except I'm having to plough through two dinners every mealtime.'

'No way!' exclaimed Pippa. 'I'm surprised at you, Maria – had you pinned for a bright spark! Why are you putting yourself through that misery? It's not rocket science! See here.' She pulled a small freezer bag from her sleeve.

'You've gotta be kidding me,' whined Maria. 'Have

you been doing that all week? How have we not seen you?!'

'Cos I'm the Queen of Cool, dufus! And besides, sometimes you two are so caught up in your own twin world, you wouldn't notice if I sat here for an entire meal with my knickers on my head!'

'Now, you think of something to distract the Jackal and I'll fly by and clear Betsy's plate into the bag and then we're all out of here. I'd rather do cola bottles and cake again tonight anyway – there's nothing decent left.'

Pippa stuffed the plastic bag back up her sleeve and slinked down the dining room to position herself ready for the swoop.

Molly looked at Maria. 'What are you going to do?' she asked urgently. Maria thought for a second and then grinned. 'Do you remember that stunt we pulled last Christmas to get out of performing at yet another boring drinks and canapés party Mum and Dad had?'

Molly paused for a moment and then the realisation of what lay ahead dawned. 'Oh no, not again, really? That took all of my acting strength and I'm not quite sure I did it justice the first time round!'

'Come oooon, Molly!' ordered Maria and rushed

over to grab a huge ugly sprout from an unsuspecting Belle Brown's plate. 'Ready?' she asked.

'Ready,' answered Molly, and as she thrust the disgusting green vegetable into her mouth, Maria started flailing her arms and screaming.

'She's choking . . . quick, somebody help! She's choking!' Maria threw her arms around Molly's waist from behind and began squeezing her hard (something she had once seen in a film), heaving in and out as convincingly as she could without actually hurting her sister. Molly meanwhile was putting on a choking display worthy of an Oscar. Between them, they were making quite a scene.

Lucinda had been watching the plot unfold, and was wondering how she could best expose their little show and get them into the most trouble. But before she had time to interfere, Mackle the Jackal was on the move, up the centre of the Ivy Room, throwing students left and right, obliterating any chair or table in her path. Then Molly, mid-splutter, to her absolute horror, saw Lucinda run over to Sister Payne, who turned and made a beeline for them.

Well, with a name like that, Story-seeker, she could only have been the school nurse, couldn't she!

As soon as the Jackal's back was turned at the other end of the dining room, Pippa was on Betsy's plate faster than you could blink, shovelling her leftovers into the bag, then out through the exit like a rat up a drainpipe.

Betsy had absolutely no idea what had happened and just sat staring at her clean plate in grateful astonishment.

Maria, seeing that their mission had been accomplished, whispered in Molly's ear, 'NOW!' and with one last convulsion, Molly expelled the enormous, amazingly untouched sprout with such violence that it hit the dining-room window and rolled down the pane, leaving a slimy trail in its wake. The room erupted into whoops and applause from the girls. Molly, still in character, collapsed in a heap on the floor gasping for breath and tearfully uttering, 'You saved me . . . you saved me.' Sister Payne had arrived in time to see the sprout make its miraculous exit and was now on her hands and knees stroking Molly's hair.

'Well done, Maria. I must say, I couldn't have done better myself.' Then she turned to the rest of the students and scolded, 'This is why you should all make time to attend my first aid club on a Monday lunchtime. You never know when disaster may strike. Let this be a lesson to you all!' And on that note, she scooped Molly up, and marched her off to the sick bay.

'Come on everyone,' exclaimed Maria with glee, although full of sympathy for Molly. 'Let's get *sprout* of here.' And the girls once again collapsed into fits of giggles.

Pippa, Maria, Daisy, Lydia, Belle – and Betsy and Autumn, who had sneaked over from Monroe to thank everyone – waited anxiously in their bedroom at Garland for Molly to get back from the san.

'Pippa, that's so clever. I've just been rolling mine up in toilet paper and stuffing it down the back of the radiator,' exclaimed Lydia in awe.

'Well, that's just brilliant, Lyds – the whole place is going to be stinking to high heaven in a week with the heat those radiators are throwing out,' sniped Maria – worried about what Molly was going through and slightly put out that Pippa had usurped her 'genius' title.

'I don't even want to admit what I've been doing,' confessed Belle, the ballet dancer, going redder by the second. 'I was so desperate. I've been putting it in a napkin too and then tucking that hideous, soggy mess up my sleeve.'

'Gross!' giggled Pippa.

'That's not the half of it – you try flushing that lot down the toilet after every meal! It doesn't all usually …well, you know, go down, without a bit of prodding!' Belle finished, mortified, and the girls exploded into laughter all over again.

'Yuk! You guys are totally disgusting!' A bedraggled Molly appeared at the doorway.

'Molly!' Maria cried out. 'Are you OK? You've been ages!'

'Well, I've been pushed and prodded in places I didn't even know existed, but I'm fine.' She shuddered and Maria squeezed her sister's shoulder in a reassuring *well done* kind of way. 'Anyway, never mind sick bay! Wasn't that totally brilliant? The best fun I've had in ages. I think I was particularly convincing that time, wasn't I?'

Maria began to roll her eyes and then checked herself. 'You were fabulous,' she said proudly.

'I don't know how to thank you all,' said Betsy, almost in tears.

'Well, it was Pippa's idea,' said Maria gallantly.

'Oh no – I just brought the bag along – you guys

did all the work with your dramatics. You might be a bit slow on the uptake about how to remedy a seemingly impossible situation, but boy do you know how to carry out a plan!' Pippa praised them.

'Well, thanks so much,' said Betsy again from the heart. 'We'd best be off before anyone discovers we're missing. First thing I'm going to do when I get back to Monroe is put in a massive order for freezer bags! See you in the morning, my friends.'

'Byeee,' the remaining group called as she and Autumn disappeared down the corridor, back to Monroe.

'We'd best get back to our rooms too,' said Belle. 'Thanks for a brilliant afternoon, girls. What will we think of next?' Lydia, Daisy and Belle hugged the Garland girls goodbye.

What next indeed, thought Maria to herself later that night when she was tucked up in bed with her laptop, writing her first blog of the term. This evening's dinner shenanigans had inspired her. *I know*, she thought to herself, a contented grin on her face. *I'll call it 'Better Sprout Than In!' Brilliant!*

There was one thing though which had stuck in her throat . . .

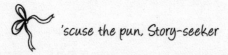

. . . about the evening's events. It was Pippa's comment that she, Maria *the brains*, had been slow on the uptake about finding a solution to the nightmare that was Mackle the Jackal and her Ivy Room patrol. Pippa was right, she had been completely useless; she'd even been eating two meals at a time, for goodness sake. That's it. From now on she'd have to sharpen up and be prepared for a crisis.

6

An Important Announcement

Maria had sneaked out of Garland super-early the following morning to deliver printed slips of paper with the 'Yours, L'Etoilette' website address and a brief description into everyone's pigeonholes. By the time 1 Alpha had reached the second hour of their technology lesson, which was the practical half of the lesson, Maria was delighted to see at least half the class secretly logging on to her website and reading her account of the dining-room rescue episode. Several of them were giggling so much, they nearly got caught by Mr West who was pacing up and down the aisles, monitoring monitors! She thought she'd better log on herself so people could see her looking too. It wouldn't do to be exposed this early in the game! Maria smiled to herself. This made ballet so much easier to stomach.

Lunch that day was fairly uneventful, given that most of the girls had now cottoned on to the fail-safe way of disposing of their unwanted leftovers. Mackle the Jackal could barely hide her frustration as she eyed up clean plate after clean plate as each girl filed past her looking smug.

'Something's going on around here!' she drawled to one of her fellow jackals. 'And I'm going to find out what it is. Them girls think they've got the better of me, but no one beats the Mackle at her own game.' And for the first time in her cooking career at L'Etoile, she retired to her office kitchen before lunch was over.

'I don't know how long we've got before Mackle busts us!' Molly said as she held her nose and emptied her two freezer bags full of disgusting brown slop into the toilet. 'She knows something's up and it's killing her. I'd even go so far as to suggest she's lost weight!'

'Fat chance! Ha!' exploded Pippa, as she flushed the loo and followed Molly back to their bedroom.

Maria looked up from her laptop as the giggling girls entered.

'Moll, there's an email here from Albie. He reckons

♥ 58 ♥

he'll be able to get here for about half-past twelve on Friday – blimey, that's tomorrow – but you'll have to sneak out and meet him up the drive somewhere. If he gets caught bringing deliveries into the school, Ruby'll be sure to have something to say about it,' she warned.

'Who's Albie?' Pippa asked.

'Molly's lifeline to Vogue and cutting-edge fashion!' Maria replied.

'Well, you don't seem to mind so much when I'm kitting you out in the latest fashions. And anyway, Mummy's always giving him little extra things to bring down for us – including extension plugs for you!' Molly retorted in annoyance. 'Albie, Pippa, is my little delivery friend. I've been placing weekly orders on www.looklikeastar.com for the last six months or so and he's never missed a drop yet. Why don't you come with me tomorrow when I pop out to meet him?'

'Sure, why not?' Pippa agreed, up for a little excitement.

'Brill!' Molly exclaimed. 'And when we get back with all the new stuff I ordered, we can have our own little fashion show . . .' Pippa opened her mouth to protest but was suddenly interrupted by a voice on the school intercom:

DING DONG

Attention all First-Year Students.

This is Madame Ruby speaking. I have a very exciting announcement for you all, so please pay attention as it involves every single one of you. There is to be a Christmas gala on the evening of Friday 13th December in the Kodak Hall. Each of you will be required to perform in front of an audience made up of parents and talent scouts from across the globe. I cannot impress upon you enough how important a platform this is to get your talent noticed and ask that you sleep on it and come up with some ideas for tomorrow's Friday Entertainment Session which, incidentally, this week will be with me and Miss Hart.

Good Night, L'Etoilettes.

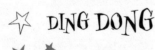

DING DONG

Molly's jaw almost hit the floor.

'Did you hear that, Mimi? Did you?' Molly screeched.

'Of course I bloomin' heard it,' Maria replied. 'We all did.'

'A Christmas gala! Oh how wonderful.' Molly was all of a daydream. 'I can't wait to invite Mum and Dad to L'Etoile.'

Maria looked over at Pippa, who appeared to be in a complete panic.

She tossed her laptop aside and sprang over to Pippa's bed. 'What's worrying you, Pips?' she enquired, concerned.

'Two things, really. I know for a fact my mum won't be able to make it, as the school where she teaches has its own Christmas production that day. They've been rehearsing for weeks. Plus, I've never really sung in front of anyone before. Not in person anyway. The internet's different – you can't see a thousand faces looking at you. What if they don't like my music, what if they don't like my voice, what if I totally clam up and no sound comes out?'

Molly, who had now come back down to earth, was at Pippa's other side, holding her hand. 'You'll be amazing, Pippa. You've got more natural talent in your little finger than the rest of us put together. And anyway, by the time I've finished your makeover, all your confidence issues will just melt away.'

'Makeover?' Pippa stammered, her big eyes searching Molly's.

Maria raised an eyebrow. 'Here we go again...can't believe it's taken you this long, Moll,' she said with a grin. 'All I can say is, brace yourself Miss Burrows, and get ready to be plucked and painted to within an inch of your life!'

'Oh, Mimi!'

'Only kidding, Moll! Pippa, my sister is nothing if not a beautificating genius. I suggest you sit back, relax and plug in to my iPod. This is going to take some time, but I guarantee you'll be totally made-up! Ha, made-up – get it? Ha!'

And with that, Molly had leapt out of bed and was busy untangling her hair straighteners. It was time to pull out all the stops and make this divine diva look like a star!

7

Beware the Wolf in Sheep's Clothing

*P*ippa, absolutely desperate for the loo – or, if the truth be known, to have another quick look at herself in the mirror since Molly's overnight transformation – had shot out of drama class as soon as the bell rang. Molly had somehow managed to tame her wild mane of black hair, leaving her looking more sleek and sophisticated than she could ever have imagined. She felt like a true superstar. In fact she was so caught up in her own thoughts that she hadn't noticed Lucinda steal away after her.

When she emerged from the cubicle, Lucinda, who was standing in front of the mirrors re-plaiting her hair, swirled round and made her jump.

'Oh!' Pippa gasped, shoving the little pink comb Molly had given her into her bag. 'You scared the life out of me. I didn't realise anyone else was in here.'

'Hello Pippa,' Lucinda began, her eyes transfixed by Pippa's. 'Actually I followed you in. I've got something for you that I didn't want the others to see.'

Pippa looked at her, at first alarmed, and then suspicious. 'For me?' she said, puzzled. 'What do you mean?'

Lucinda reached into her designer Prada bag and pulled out a white envelope with a yellow and blue logo in the corner.

UNIVERSAL
MUSIC
PUBLISHING

And in the centre of the envelope was written:

PIPPA BURROWS

L'ETOILE, SCHOOL FOR STARS

She thrust it in Pippa's direction. 'Daddy was given this to pass on to you.'

Pippa, totally bewildered, stared at the envelope in silence, all manner of things going through her head – mostly, *what is Lucifette playing at?*

'Aren't you going to open it then?' Lucinda said impatiently.

'Right ... yeah ... erm ... what is it?' Pippa replied, gingerly turning the envelope over in her hands, as if it contained some kind of ticking bomb.

'Oh, just open it and find out,' snapped Lucinda, in total frustration.

Just then, Belle Brown and dancer Amanda Lloyd, both Garland girls, burst in, singing at the tops of their voices. They stopped dead at the unusual sight of Lucinda talking to Pippa.

Their entrance seemed to send Lucinda into a fluster. 'As I was saying, Pippa ... if you could just, er . . . help me pitch my harmonies for Friday's Entertainment Session that would be great. I just can't seem to get them right. Have you got a sec to go to the Royal Albert rooms now?' she asked.

'Um ... sure,' Pippa replied, still bewildered. Before she knew it, Lucinda had grabbed her by the arm and whisked her off down the corridor to one of the piano rooms, where Pippa tore open the envelope and read:

Dear Miss Burrows,

It has been brought to my attention via the Marciano family that you are a lady of some considerable vocal and songwriting talent.

I understand that as an attendee of L'Etoile, you have aspirations to become a singing sensation and having listened to some of your material through your web page, I, and my team here at Universal Music, feel that we could work together to develop your talent and potentially launch you onto the world's stage.

I would very much like you to come to my London Office at Universal Music Publishing for a meeting on Friday 13th December at 5 p.m. I will make all the necessary travel arrangements and send a driver to collect you from school in the morning and return you the same evening. All I ask is that you clear this with the relevant staff members and confirm your attendance with me via the Marciano family as I shall be working with Mr Marciano for the rest of the week finding artists to score for his next blockbuster.

Yours sincerely,

Emmett Fuller

President, Universal Music Publishing

Pippa looked up at Lucinda, aghast at what she had just read. 'W-what the . . .?' She just didn't understand.

'Oh, give it here.' Lucinda snatched the letter and scanned it. 'Wow!' she said, 'that's quite an invitation! Shame it clashes with the Christmas gala though.'

Pippa's face drained of colour. She'd never be allowed to get out of that one. Miss Hart would never agree to her absence, not with all that was at stake. What a decision – a real *crossroads moment*. Which route should she take? Should she put all her eggs in one basket and head up to Universal Music, or take her chances and perform to dozens of world-famous talent scouts in attendance at the gala – but risk being outshone by the nineteen other girls in her year who would also be performing as if their lives depended on it?

'I know what you're thinking,' snapped Lucinda again. 'But really, Pippa – it's a no-brainer. Opportunities like this don't come along every day – or perhaps they do for the great Pippa Burrows?'

'Oh no!' Pippa exclaimed. 'I truly am so, so grateful for this, Lucinda. Really I am. It's just . . .'

'Just what? Just that you'd prefer to sing in some little school concert for your family – or that you'd like to change your family's fortune forever by becoming a worldwide superstar? I know what I'd do if I was given such a golden opportunity. Do you think these kinds of offers grow on trees, Pippa?'

Pippa shrugged. 'How did they even find out about me in the first place?' she asked again. 'I just can't quite believe that they would be interested. They must see thousands of artists all the time. What makes me so special?'

'Because of me, stupid,' Lucinda spat, exasperated. 'As the letter says, Mr Fuller is working with Daddy to produce a soundtrack for his latest film. He's at the house all the time, and last weekend when I went home, the whole 'U' Music team was there. They asked me who was the most talented star in my year and I, of course, told them all about you, Pippa.'

'Oh, Lucinda – did you really?' Pippa said, not quite believing what she was hearing. 'I'm so sorry – I had you all wrong. Now I see that you have just been very misunderstood. Wait until I tell the others how wonderful you've been to me.'

Lucinda immediately turned serious. 'I wouldn't do that if I were you, Pippa,' she warned. 'Especially not the twins. You know how desperately Molly wants stardom for herself. One word from her to the great Mr Fitzfoster and he'll be straight on the phone to Emmett Fuller asking for the same audition. Do you really want to risk that?'

Pippa immediately felt upset. Molly wouldn't do that to her. Not her dear friend Molly. But it was too late. The doubt had already crept in.

'No, I s'pose not,' she responded.

'And anyway,' Lucinda continued, 'you've got me to talk things through with and rehearse with. I've seen a million of these sorts of auditions and can tell you exactly what to expect.'

Mentally, Pippa felt as if she'd gone ten rounds in a boxing ring. Even though she had in her hand a letter, displaying the facts in black and white, something didn't quite add up. Here was Lucinda, the enemy, standing before her, giving her the chance of a lifetime – and not only that, but offering her friendship, support and to coach her through it.

'Thank you,' she said meekly, beaten into submission by the one girl she had said she would never let get the better of her. She pushed the nagging feelings of suspicion to one side and decided to put her faith in Lucinda. What choice did she have?

'Oh, but what about Miss Hart? She'll never let me miss the Christmas gala.'

Lucinda paused. 'I wouldn't tell the teachers either.'

'What? I can't do that. I'll be expelled!' answered Pippa in a complete panic.

'There's more ways than being honest to get out of school,' Lucinda replied. 'And you said yourself, they'll never let you go willingly. How about this for an idea? What if Miss Hart receives a phone call from your mother the morning of the gala saying that your Uncle Harry has been taken ill and that she is sending a car to collect you immediately? What could she possibly say in answer to that? So long as the car turns up as promised, she'll have to let you go.'

Pippa's face fell. 'But my mother wouldn't lie for me – and neither would Uncle Harry,' she protested, feeling as though the whole plan was falling down around her ankles.

'Oh Pippa, Pippa,' Lucinda taunted. 'Where is your ingenuity? Where is your courage? Where is your brain? Do you think any of the great stars of stage and screen made it without a little bit of cunning along the way?'

Pippa felt completely out of her depth and, for a second, sorry for all the mean things she'd said about Sally Sudbury. That poor girl didn't have a hope of having a mind of her own with Lucinda around. She really was so persuasive.

'It won't really be your mum phoning – it'll be me on the other end of the phone – pretending to be your mum,' Lucinda said.

'But you don't even know what my mum sounds like,' stammered Pippa.

'And Miss Hart does? Oh please, Pippa – do you honestly think that Miss Hart is going to remember what your mother sounds like from the two-second conversation she had with her on the drive on the first day of term and a couple of chats on the phone? Of course she won't! If I put my mind to it, I can convince anyone of just about anything,' Lucinda finished ominously.

Pippa took the letter back from her and stared at it. The elation, confusion and now fear that she felt about what all this deception meant made her eyes prick with tears. She fought hard to hold them back, not wanting to appear weak in front of Lucinda. As she read the words over and over, they seemed to be swirling in front of her as if to create a big black hole in the centre of the page. Was this where she was heading if she followed Lucinda's advice? A big black hole of lies and deceit? Or would there be light at the end of the tunnel – a singing career for her and financial security for her family – no more night job for Mum – and a real music studio for Uncle Harry?

'Listen,' Lucinda broke into her thoughts. 'You have a think about it, but take my advice and tell no one! Meet me back here during study time tomorrow at four o'clock and let me know what you've decided. As I said, I'm more than happy to help you prepare. In fact, do you have a CD of your full vocal and backing tracks on you now that I can familiarise myself with tonight?'

'Sure,' said Pippa, quite overwhelmed by Lucinda's attention to detail and enthusiasm. And she scrabbled around in her rucksack. She handed over the two discs, which she'd been carrying around for any spare gala rehearsal time.

'Great, I'll have a listen to everything tonight and tomorrow we'll pick the best one for you to perform. I'll even learn it so that we can rehearse together tomorrow.' Lucinda turned on her heel and left the piano room.

'Oh my goodness, oh my goodness,' was all that was running through Pippa's mind as she ran off to the library to meet the girls for study. What had just happened? How could she keep this huge secret? All being well, she'd come back and surprise everyone with a signed record contract. And if the worst came to the worst, no one would ever know she'd failed. She needed to keep it simple in her mind, all the better for the truth to remain between her and one other – even if it was Lucinda. Too many cooks spoil the broth and all that.

8

Hook, Line and Sinker

When Pippa entered the library looking for the twins for study time, she didn't see Lucinda deep in whispered discussions with Sally in the fiction section.

'Hook, line and sinker!' Lucinda snorted to Sally, who was sneaking a brownie she'd pinched from yesterday's pudding selection. 'Wow, I'm good, brilliant even. She fell for every word. There's no way she won't turn up tomorrow ready to rehearse. I even got her to hand over all her tracks!' She flashed the silver CDs.

'She didn't, did she?' Sally frowned through a mouthful of chocolate sponge. 'Oh, Lucinda, I'm not sure. I've got a bad feeling about this. What if she tells someone?'

'Do shut up, Sal – she wouldn't dare now – not after the number I've done on her.' Lucinda hated it when Sally questioned her mastery. 'My idea of saying that a driver would be sent for her was the icing on the cake in terms of giving the whole plan authenticity. I'll just arrange that with Daddy's secretary and make out I need to be picked up and dropped back that night. She's too scared of me to ask any questions or run anything past Dad since she forgot my hair appointment. When Miss Hart sees a car arrive for Pipsy she won't even question that her family haven't really sent it to take her straight to the hospital. I am, officially, a genius!'

Sally, covered in crumbs, glanced up at her and agreed. Part of her wished she could be so clever and so without conscience.

But the truth was, Story-seeker, that Sally Sudbury, no matter how much she tried to bury it, had a good heart.

It wasn't her fault that she had been born into a life of subservience to the bullying Lucinda Marciano. She'd never known anything different and Sally had quickly learned that it was far better to be on Lucinda's side than not. There had been one time at their old school when Sally had, from nowhere, taken a shot at goal during a crucial netball match, something, which is nigh-on impossible for the Goal-Keeper to do, and it had flown through the net, like a knife through butter. It was just one of those moments in life where you see a target and go for it, just knowing that it's going to work and, boy, did Sally succeed. The whole team, and most of the spectators, came running on to the court to hug her, as the perfectly timed goal coincided with the final whistle. For those two or three minutes, Sally had finally felt what it was like to be popular, to be adored and to be praised for having talent.

As you can imagine, Lucinda, who was team captain and held the shooter position of Goal Attack, was incandescent by the time they got back to the bus. How dare Sally steal even a second of her limelight? Who did she think she was? Well, it would be the last time! And Lucinda had been the vilest of the vile to Sally for the rest of term.

'You're quiet tonight, Pips,' said Molly, doodling on her jotter.

'Huh?' Pippa looked up. 'Just tired, Moll.' She yawned. 'Drama really took it out of me today. I just don't get Shakespeare.'

'I did *Romeo and Juliet* last year and still have all my notes,' said Maria. 'So just shout if you need a hand.' Jokingly, she held out a hand to Pippa.

Pippa felt tearful again. She really did love the twins. They were always looking out for her. Molly had made her look like a princess and Maria treated her as an equal, which she knew wasn't a compliment Maria gave lightly.

As the supper bell went, Pippa thought she'd keep her news to herself overnight and then decide what to do in the morning. Who knew what might happen before her meeting with Lucinda? Maybe she'd get lucky and Maria and Molly would somehow guess why she was so quiet. Highly unlikely though, she realised, surprised by the disappointment she felt. She almost wanted to get caught – then there'd be no choice to make.

The weekly Friday Entertainment Session had now been allocated as rehearsal time for the first-year students to make sure they were as prepared as possible for their big moment on 13th December – or Doomsday as some had coined it when they'd worked out the day fell on a Friday. Parcels of pink knickers arrived in armfuls from superstitious parents, for their girls to ward off any Friday 13th bad luck.

The first-years were spread around the Kodak Hall with Madame Ruby at the helm spelling out what this golden opportunity meant for them all.

'A moment's hush now, L'Etoilettes. I need not impress on you how important your choice of performance is. Friday 13th is the day when talent scouts and critics flock to L'Etoile from all over the world to see you, the new crop of up-and-coming stars. You each have a very short time to shine and impress. They will be watching your every move. May I also take this opportunity to say that you need not only sound your best, but you must also look your best.'

As Lucinda shot Sally a scornful glance, Molly glowed with pride as she looked at Pippa who sat there, groomed to breathtaking perfection.

'I have made arrangements for the very best hair and make-up people – or the glamsquad as we refer to them in the industry – to be on standby that day. It will, however, be entirely up to you to make sure that you look fabulous.'

Betsy Harris winced and whispered to Autumn in a panic, 'What am I going to wear? I've already been through my whole wardrobe this morning and there's nothing in it which will even slightly pass for fabulous!'

'Don't worry, Betsy,' Molly whispered over her shoulder. 'Come over to Garland on Sunday afternoon and we'll find you something. Pips and I have just picked up a new order from Albie. There'll definitely be something for you there. And Faye Summers is a complete star with the sewing machine – she'll be able to take anything in or up for you. She's totally going to be the next Vivienne Westwood!'

Blonde-haired, blue-eyed Faye, who was sitting a few rows in front, too close to Lucinda for her liking, turned round and winked at Betsy.

Lucinda rolled her eyes and sneered. 'Yes, I'm sure she can do wonders with a pillowcase for you, Betsy – no one will ever know – NOT! Just make sure you send it to the laundry first, Faye . . . Betsy won't look great wearing an outfit with your dribble on it!'

Maria fizzed with anger. 'Put a sock in it, Marciano. And I suppose you'll be having something flown in from Milan.' Lucinda smirked at Maria and nodded in agreement.

'Oh, that's too bad. Mum says it's Paris or nothing this season,' Maria shot back.

Lucinda pouted in her direction then turned her back on her. She never seemed to answer Maria back. And quite rightly too – Maria's razor tongue was at its sharpest against her enemies.

'And so, my L'Etoilettes, I leave you now in the capable hands of my deputy, Miss Hart and her team,' Madame Ruby said.

She exited stage left and through the back entrance to the theatre.

'Off she goes . . .' giggled Molly, 'back into make-up for the forty-fourth time today.' Her classmates roared.

'Girls!' exclaimed Miss Hart. 'May we all share the joke?' She looked expectantly at Molly and her gaggle of friends. For once they were as quiet as mice.

'Right then,' she continued, uninterrupted. 'Time for you to split up into your performance categories. Instrumentals – you will be with our Musical Director, Mr Potts, to the right-hand side of the stage by the piano. Actresses, you will be with Miss Fleming at the back of the hall to my left.'

The girls started to grab their things and manoeuvre.

'Wait a second, ladies . . . please let me finish,' she scolded. 'Dancers, you will be under the excellent supervision of Miss Seminova at the other side of the hall to my right, and singers, you will be with me down here. Best of luck to you all.'

Twenty girls started scrambling in four different directions, desperate to get to their respective teacher first for advice. Or should that be nineteen girls, leaving one very confused Faye Summers still sitting in the middle of the theatre alone. She put her hand up. 'Miss, Miss,' she called out to Miss Hart, her voice rising anxiously.

'Oh Faye, I'm so sorry. I quite forgot. We would very much like you to style the whole event.' Fashion Faye's mouth dropped open in shock.

'As you know,' Miss Hart continued, the other girls now listening intently, 'L'Etoile usually only takes on performance students, but with your brilliant flair for textile design, Madame Ruby was only too happy to host one of the country's budding fashion designers.'

Faye beamed as there were a few whoops of congratulations from the Garland girls. Lucinda elbowed Sally spitefully as she started to clap, and waved her hand in the air for attention.

'Erm . . . Miss Hart, my mom is sending my stage costume over from Mil . . . er . . . Paris.' Maria noticed with glee how the very stupid Lucinda had taken note of her lies about Paris. 'Will I be subjected to one of Miss Summer's designs? I'm not sure Mom would be too pleased about that.'

Faye looked wounded but not surprised, while an irate Miss Hart tried to smother her frustration with the favoured celebrity student.

'That, Lucinda dear, is a question for Madame Ruby. I very much doubt that you will be eligible for any special treatment regarding costumes ... but I will of course raise your query at the next staff meeting.'

Slightly unprofessionally, Miss Hart hoped that Faye would have the opportunity to dress Lucinda in any way she deemed fit, but somehow felt that Madame Ruby would sooner come to the gala without her lipstick than risk upsetting Mrs Marciano! Lucinda gave a triumphant, smug nod.

The vocalists, consisting of Pippa, Alice, Sofia, Corine, Lucinda and the divinely named Charlotte Kissimee, crowded around Miss Hart, who was handing out sheet music.

'What are you going to sing, Pippa?' asked Sofia Vincenzi.

Pippa shot Lucinda a guilty look and mumbled something about not having completely decided yet. Sofia Vincenzi was an opera student of Italian descent.

While it would take years for her voice to mature to a true operatic standard, she already possessed the most exquisite soprano range and was a definite contender among the singers. She had been born in Venice to a theatrical family, but had moved to England when her father, Antonio Russo, a world-famous Italian chef, had come over about ten years previously, to open some very exclusive Italian restaurants.

Sofia babbled on. 'Charlotte and I would LOVE to do "The Flower Duet" from the opera *Lakmé*. But I'm not sure if we'll be allowed to perform together.'

Charlotte Kissimee and Sofia were roommates at Monroe and had been inseparable since their arrival at L'Etoile. Their beautiful voices could be heard at all hours, floating around the school.

'That's a great idea!' said Pippa. 'I totally love that song – it's the one from the advert, isn't it?' she asked, desperate to keep the focus away from her.

'Si!' bubbled Sofia, brimming with excitement. 'Charlotte and I have already been practising it!'

'So we've all heard,' growled Lucinda, unimpressed.

Miss Hart, who had been sitting back, listening to the girls' ideas with interest, entered the conversation. 'I'll have to check with Madame Ruby, ladies, but I think that song would combine your voices beautifully and really show off your abilities. Why don't you put something together and we'll see what she says.'

Sofia and Charlotte hugged each other and ran off to a quiet corner to practice.

Alice Parry, who had been nearly as quiet as Pippa, suddenly jumped up. 'I've got it!' she declared, nearly knocking Corine off her chair. 'Ooops – sorry, Corine.'

'I'm gonna . . . going . . . to sing Wouldn't It Be Loverly from *My Fair Lady*. I was in that at my old school and it was such fun. I'll have to work on it, Miss – but I fink – I think – that I could do a really good cockney accent. What do you fink?'

Pippa had to muffle a giggle. Alice's family had come from humble beginnings in the East End of London, but thanks to their very canny investments, the Parrys now owned Parry Parks – which consisted of most of the car-park properties in central England. Alice's father, Big Al Parry, was determined that his daughter should not be held back by his lack of social know-how and had sent Alice to every finishing school and elocution specialist in the country in an attempt to disguise her cockney roots. The result of all this training was that unlike Pippa, who understood and accepted that no amount of success would make her sound like the Queen, Alice was convinced that years of elocution lessons had banished her cockney accent forever.

'Wonderful idea,' agreed Miss Hart. 'It's perfect for you, Alice – I know you'll do it complete justice.'

'All she wants is a room somewhere. . .' sang Lucinda maliciously. 'But who's she kidding? This is one flower girl who'll never pass for a lady!' She turned sniggering to the rest of the group. 'Who's she kidding?'

A mortified Alice scurried off with her laptop to download the lyrics.

Miss Hart turned her attention to cruel Lucinda, to put a stop to the taunting.

'And what, may I ask, have you come up with, Miss Marciano?' she said, coldly.

Lucinda was a little taken aback by Miss Hart's tone. How dare she talk to her like that in front of her classmates? But the truth was that Miss Hart had caught her unawares, as she hadn't planned far enough ahead to think of a response to this question. She planned to steal one of Pippa's songs, but she could hardly say that. Thinking on her feet, and not too successfully, she said that she was in the middle of writing something spectacular. 'You can't hurry perfection,' Lucinda drawled. 'I shall come and see you separately with my chosen piece, Miss Hart.'

Miss Hart eyeballed her and then nodded in annoyance. Looking around her group she summarised, 'Right then – so that's you, Lucinda, and Pippa who need to come back to me with a solid idea ASAP. As it is, you only have three weeks to rehearse, so time really is of the essence. I'm happy to make some suggestions if you are short of ideas, girls.' Pippa looked away in shame and Lucinda reddened at the insinuation that she had come unprepared.

'Anyone else – oh yes – Corine.' Miss Hart looked at her.

Corine didn't flinch. '"Memory", from the musical *Cats*,' she said. 'I've some terrific ideas for a catsuit which I'll speak to Faye about.'

'Oh pullllease . . .' groaned Lucinda again, incensed by the idea that Corine would look simply fabulous in a catsuit.

'OK, L'Etoilettes . . . that's enough for today. Pippa, Lucinda, I shall expect to hear from you imminently. As for the rest of you, well done, girls. I'm really very impressed with your efforts so far and look forward to hearing you all in rehearsal.'

As she disbanded her group of vocalists, Mr Potts, with one arm bent at the elbow, his hand resting on his waist, and the other hand flailing around – looking very much like a *teapott* – did the same with his musicians. The pianists, Maria, Autumn and Betsy, had all chosen classical pieces which would show off their command of the keys. Daisy had selected the famous bassoon solo from *Peter and the Wolf*, Lara had chosen a very noisy drum piece which was slightly too rocky for Mr Potts' old-fashioned taste but a superb example of rhythm, and Lydia was to send everyone to Dreamland with Johannes Brahms's masterpiece, Wiegenlied, known to everyone as Brahms's Lullaby.

The dancers, Belle, Heavenly, Amanda and Elizabeth had discussed the styles they would most like to perform under the guidance of Miss Seminova. It was slightly more difficult to discuss which pieces these would be, as each wanted to choreograph her own routine. These four girls had perhaps the most work to do in the coming weeks and had left the hall early for some time at the barre in the Bolshoi Suite.

Last, but by no means least, were the actresses – Molly, Nancy and Sally.

Sally had mentioned something about reciting

one of her own poems, which had raised an eyebrow or two among the girls, but Miss Fleming seemed delighted by her originality.

Nancy had chosen Shakespeare's monologue by Lady Macbeth after she's just helped her husband to murder the king. This had slightly annoyed Molly as she had been prepared to do Juliet's 'Wherefore art thou Romeo?' soliloquy from *Romeo and Juliet*, but when Nancy had got in there first with *Macbeth*, she quickly had to change tack.

'Oh no!' cried Maria later that night, as Molly recounted who was doing what among the drama group.

'I know, WATC eh?!' Molly exclaimed in a huff.

'WATC?' asked Maria, confused. Even she sometimes struggled to translate every Mollyism.

'What are the chances?' Molly cried, wondering why she couldn't work that out.

'So what are you going to do now, then?' Maria said.

'Well, I explained to Miss Fleming what had happened and that I need a bit of time to come up with something. I was thinking though about doing that split-personality monologue I did for my final exam.'

Maria exploded into laughter . . . remembering Molly on that huge stage all by herself, lit by a single spotlight, jumping up and down pretending to be five different personalities. She'd been so convincing that their mother had even taken her to the doctor the following week just to make sure that Molly didn't actually have a multiple personality disorder!

'Oh Molly – that would be superb and will blow everyone else out of the water. Shakespeare, Schmakespeare. Wait till they get a load of Molly the schoolgirl . . . and Marilyn, Queen of Hollywood, and Mary the Welsh shepherdess!' Tears of joy were rolling down Maria's face.

'Don't forget Marlene the school teacher and Mildred the murderer!' Both girls giggled as they reminisced and Molly acted out little snippets on her bed.

'Yo! What's so funny?' asked Pippa as she arrived back, collapsing onto her bed.

'Oh do it for her, Moll – pulllease!' pleaded Maria.

'Not now, I'm pooped and we haven't really got time before bed.'

'How'd you go, Pips?' asked Molly through a mouthful of toothpaste.

'Oh, you know . . . not bad,' Pippa said coyly.

'Not bad – what are you talking about?' Molly

asked in surprise. 'I would have thought you, out of everyone, would have had the easiest decision. You've written so many fab songs. Any one of them's a winner IMB.'

Pippa threw Maria a confused glance. 'In my book,' Maria translated.

'Ah, thanks, Moll. I just need to have a think which will be best.'

Pippa felt awful about keeping a secret from her BFFs. As she put her head on her pillow, she knew she had some hard thinking to do before her meeting with Lucinda in the music room tomorrow afternoon. Once she'd agreed to accept her help, there'd be no going back. She just hoped her friends would forgive her in the long run, once she came back to L'Etoile with a signed music contract in her hands.

9

Life's a Dream

*L*ucinda was already waiting in the music room when Pippa arrived. Poor Pippa hadn't had a wink of sleep and felt exhausted.

'I was beginning to think you weren't coming,' snapped Lucinda, her usual charming self.

'Yeah, sorry, got held up,' Pippa mumbled.

Lucinda looked at Pippa thoughtfully. She couldn't help but notice how naturally attractive Pippa was – and perhaps even more so now with her face betraying a certain vulnerability. There was no denying it – this girl was a threat, and much better out of the way.

'Well, Burrows, are you in or out?' demanded Lucinda.

Pippa took a deep breath. 'I'm in,' she answered quietly, and as she did so it felt as if the sun had chosen that moment to disappear behind a cloud on purpose.

'Don't look too happy about it!' cried Lucinda. 'I'm about to hand you the keys to the rest of your life!'

Now it was Pippa's turn to study her new partner in crime. Lucinda was stunning but had a permanently spiteful look – even when she was trying to be nice, her face was pinched and mean.

'So what's the plan then?' Pippa gathered herself.

'I'm glad you asked. I've added a bit since we last spoke to make sure that you're not putting all your eggs in one basket,' Lucinda went on.

Pippa raised an eyebrow – was this girl really trying to help? It was all getting a bit much now.

'I've had a long think to see how we can work this so that you don't completely miss out on showcasing your talent at the gala while you're up in London schmoozing Mr Fuller.'

'Go on . . .' Pippa murmured hesitantly.

'I think that I should sing one of your songs, Pippa.'

And there it was – the trade-off that Pippa had known there would be behind all this kindness, but hadn't so far managed to foresee.

'One of my songs? One of the songs I've written?'

'Yep.' Lucinda jumped in quickly while she had Pippa on the hop. 'I listened to all of your tracks last night and there's one which really stands out from the rest. I think I could do it real justice at the gala. What have you got to lose? At least the audience will get to hear it – even if you're not there singing it yourself. It'll get your songwriting noticed.'

Pippa's mind was reeling. No one else had ever sung any of her songs. She'd hoped to reveal them one by one, as and when each was ready to be heard – but then again, at this moment she was completely terrified about singing in front of a huge audience. This could be an easy way out for her. She felt she was losing control of the situation.

'Which one do you want to sing?' she asked, her voice trembling slightly.

'"Life's a Dream",' Lucinda said without hesitation.

Pippa gasped. '"Life's a Dream"? Oh no, Lucinda. Really, that track is private – I didn't even realise it was on the CD I gave you – it really shouldn't have been. No one's heard that one yet. It's not even ready!'

'Life's a Dream' was the first song she had ever written. It summed up every single one of her hopes and fears and was the most personal of all her tracks. She had to try and put Lucinda off.

'Er . . . I'm not sure that one . . . I mean . . . that's so obviously about someone who comes from nothing . . . I'm not sure it'll suit your . . .'

'Nonsense,' Lucinda snarled. 'It'll be perfect . . . the irony of the words against me singing will give it the edge it needs. If you sang it, people would just pity you . . . if I sing it, my story of fortune and glory will bring it to life. You're the girl at the start of the song – I'm the prize. I'm the aspiration here.'

Pippa gasped again, fighting back the tears.

'Look, the way I see it is that you have two options. Number one – you take the chance of a one-to-one audition with Mr Fuller at Universal Music, or number two – you take your chances against the rest of the pack here at the Christmas gala. I can't understand why it isn't blatantly obvious what to do!'

'I know, I know,' bleated Pippa. 'I just always dreamed of having the confidence to sing my songs in front of an audience myself – and now it'll be you singing them.'

'So what's your point, Pippa? I only suggested this to help you out!' said Lucinda. 'Forget I even mentioned it. There are much better songs I can sing anyway.'

'No, no . . . I didn't mean . . . it's fine, really, Lucinda. I'm OK with you singing "Life's a Dream". Want to have a practice now? Maybe I can give you a few pointers.'

'Sure,' grinned Lucinda, triumphantly. 'We can rehearse together and I'll give you the low-down on old Fuller so you're fully briefed. Come on – we've got half an hour before supper.'

And so it was that Lucinda Marciano and Pippa Burrows set the wheels of deceit in motion.

10

Rehearsals and Deceit

The next few weeks whizzed by in a flurry of theatrical activity. Perhaps more run off her feet than most was Faye Summers. Madame Ruby had of course said that both Lucinda and Sally could wear whatever Mrs Marciano had selected for them in Paris, but that still left seventeen other girls turning up at Faye's door day and night.

In a desperate attempt for Faye's roommate, Alice Parry to be allowed to sleep without interruption, Miss Coates, the housemistress, had cleared out one of the large storage rooms at Garland so that Faye could relocate to a place where she could eat, sleep and drink costume design. Alice was sad to be losing her best friend, but equally delighted that she could rehearse, trade tuck with the other girls and sleep in peace.

Maria's blog was getting more hits than ever with all the details she was managing to glean about the gala. The first few weeks of publication had been a bit slow as it took a while for word to get round that there was an anonymous blogger in their midst. Now, though, it was *the* place to go for up-to-the-minute information about the show, rehearsal tips, rehearsal-room schedules and gossip. As Maria could play the piano piece she'd chosen standing on her head, she had plenty of time to make everything and everyone her business. If you looked closely enough, you would have seen her everywhere, ducking down behind desks, creeping behind bookcases in the library, listening in to anything that could feather her 'scoop'. She'd had a great response to her headlines:

'Hair Curly or Straight – the Big Debate'
'Music Room Battles – Use it or Lose it!'
'Tonsillitis Strikes Gala Stars – Top Up Your
  Vitamin C'
'Mystery Midnight Rehearser Revealed'
'Sequin Shortage Threatens Costume Completion'

'You're so clever, Mimi,' said Molly as she finished reading that morning's update entitled **'No More Nerves: How to Fight the Fright!'**

'But I do feel bad that we have to wait for Pippa to go off to morning rehearsal before we can talk about the blog. Do you think we can bring her in on it soon?'

'I just don't know,' confessed Maria, who had been feeling equally guilty that she was keeping a secret from Pippa. 'I don't know what to do about telling her. We agreed before we came, that no matter who we met, we'd keep this to ourselves rather than risk being discovered. It just works much better as an anonymous blog. People are more inclined to contact *Yours, L'Etoilette* with their thoughts if they don't know who's on the receiving end.'

Molly looked thoughtful. 'I s'pose you're right. Hadn't considered the email contribution side of things. That anonymous address you set up is a stroke of genius, BTW,' Molly continued. 'You were right about students needing an outlet to vent their feelings, or just to ask for help. Has anything new come in from anyone today?'

'Oh, good point, Moll. Haven't had a chance to check it yet,' Maria answered as she logged on to haveyoursay@letoile.co.uk.

She scrolled down about eight new messages – one from Faye asking Yours, L'Etoilette to put up a notice calling for any students who had not yet come to her for their final fittings to do so by the end of the day. With only two days to go until the gala, she was nearly at breaking point with the number of alterations she still had to make. Then there was another one from Alice Parry, asking Yours, L'Etoilette to ask if anyone had some silk flowers she could borrow for her *My Fair Lady* hat.

'Nothing particularly exciting,' Maria commented as she uploaded the student requests onto the main blog. 'It's amazing, isn't it, how much faith people put in Yours, L'Etoilette to fulfil their requests when they've no idea who's responsible.'

'That's because you've been so helpful, Mimi. No sooner do they ask, than their requests appear for the whole school to see.' Maria felt proud.

You see, Story-seeker, to all intents and purposes, she was there primarily to help and secondly to have fun, but never at anyone's expense. She was there to provide the facts, not fiction.

'Hold on a sec, Moll – look at this one!'

Molly looked up from her laptop. 'Who's it from?'

'Well, that's just it. It's from a totally random email address – not a standard student@l'etoile address.'

Molly tossed her laptop to one side and leapt over to her sister.

'This one here,' Maria pointed. 'From email@ starservice.com.'

Both the girls waited patiently for the email to open and pored over its odd contents:

To: haveyoursay@letoile.co.uk

From: email@starservice.com

Date: Wednesday 11th December – 7:04 a.m.

One little rabbit new to the scene

Met another who wanted to reign supreme

Like one in the headlights,

She'd follow her blind

What happened to that rabbit, we'll find out in time.

Maria was puzzled. Was it a joke? Or a riddle? Either way, it wasn't a very nice message – more of a threat, to be honest. One thing Maria was confident about was that she'd get to the bottom of it – this mystery writer was no match for *Yours, L'Etoilette!*

'Molly, I'm not really sure what this means at the moment. Look, let's give it some thought and talk about it tonight. One thing I would say though – let's keep this to ourselves for now. No one's supposed to know I'm the blogger, remember, and seeing as we've no idea who sent this, if we start asking questions, we might just ask the wrong person and then my cover will be completely blown.'

'OK, Mimi, but I have to say it's a bit weird. It feels like a warning or a threat or something. What if someone's trying to tell you something serious? It's totally up to us to figure this thing out. Eeek, I've got a RBF about this one.'

'Don't worry. We'll work it out – when have I ever let you and one of your Really Bad Feelings down?'

Molly threw her arms around her twin and planted a big kiss on the top of her head. 'What a team! Come on – we'd better get to class. We've got history this morning and old Butter-boots is gunning for me after my disastrous essay last week!' Maria sighed at her hopeless sibling and followed her out of the dorm.

Geography followed history and needless to say neither twin had been able to concentrate on what they were supposed to be doing. By the time they got to drama after lunch, Molly was so consumed with visions of baby rabbits running to their doom in blinding headlights that she was practically in tears.

'Maria! Have you thought any more about who might have sent that horrible email this morning – and, more importantly, who it might be about? The more I think about it, the more I think someone's really in trouble,' Molly whispered during improvisation.

'No!' Maria whispered back, feeling like a failure. She hated to be puzzled by things. 'There's always the possibility that it's a complete wind-up, Moll, by someone who's jealous of the blog.'

'Molly and Maria Fitzfoster!' Miss Fleming boomed. 'If I meant you to use this session for a gossip, you'd be tucked up in your dorm rooms! Now split up and show me how a tree would move in a storm!'

Maria rolled her eyes as Pippa grabbed her hand and started encouraging her to flail around. 'What play are we doing this week?' Maria chuckled. '*Willows in the Wind*?' Pippa managed to smother her giggles by pretending to splutter out the noise the wind would make.

Drama dissolved into individual study time and the first-year students ran off to their respective rehearsal rooms. The academic subjects like history and geography were at the bottom of the pile until the gala was over. They were on a forty-eight-hour countdown to Friday 13th December and all the girls were determined to do the best they could for themselves, their families and their futures.

There was one girl, however, who, as you know, Story-seeker, was more nervous than the rest, faced with the audition of her life on Friday.

Lucinda had surreptitiously thrust a note into Pippa's hand as she passed her in the supper queue that evening, requesting an extra meeting with her before English on Thursday morning to finalise plans for Friday. Apart from their rehearsals together, Pippa had done her level best to keep out of Lucinda's way the past three weeks since they'd become co-conspirators. The whole thing had stuck in her throat but she felt helpless to change events when there was the possibility of a record deal at the end of it. It had been so difficult to keep sneaking away from the twins early every morning – pretending to have some meeting with Miss Hart, or a rehearsal with Mr Potts. She couldn't actually believe the twins didn't suspect something. The truth was that the twins couldn't believe their luck that Pippa was so busy every morning before class, as it meant they had about fifteen minutes to themselves in the dorm to update the blog and go through the *Yours, L'Etoilette* emails. Pippa couldn't work out if the twins were just distracted by their own performances at the gala, or too caught up in twinsville to ask her any probing questions. Either way, she felt a little bit disappointed that they hadn't taken more of an interest.

You see what secrets between friends can do, Story-seeker?

Pippa once again entered the music room to find Lucinda sitting on the piano stool scribbling a note.

'You took your time – we only have ten minutes before the bell for morning lessons,' snapped Lucinda.

'Right. I'll talk, you listen. Tomorrow at ten o'clock, I'm going to phone Miss Hart from my mobile pretending to be your mother to explain about your Uncle Harry being taken ill and let her know that the family is sending a car to collect you at eleven o'clock.' Pippa just stared at Lucinda, feeling sick with nerves.

'Then I imagine old Hart will come to technology class and pull you out to explain what's happened. You will need to dig deep and appear distraught at the thought of dear Uncle Harry being poorly.' Pippa's heart sank, imagining what she'd do if she ever did receive that kind of horrendous information. It would rip her world apart.

'Pippa!' Lucinda said. 'Are you listening to me?'

'Yes!' Pippa said. 'It's just not going to be that easy, Lucinda. Lying doesn't come naturally to me.'

Lucinda threw her a spiteful look. 'It's a good job one of us is on the ball enough to launch your career then, isn't it?' she retorted. 'You should rush back to the dorm and pack a couple of things with Miss Hart to make it look authentic. You won't have to worry about bumping into Dumb and Dumber . . .

Lucinda's favourite nickname
for the Fitzfoster twins

. . . as they'll be safely tucked away in class. Then just go out and wait somewhere quietly for the car to arrive. I shouldn't imagine Miss Hart will let you out of her sight so you're going to have to keep up the act the whole time you're with her. Just one extra thing though.'

Pippa looked up at her in disbelief. 'I can't do any more!' she protested.

Lucinda thrust a piece of paper into Pippa's

hand. 'You need to make sure you copy this note in your handwriting and give it to Miss Hart before you leave. Ask her to make sure she gives it to me urgently.'

Pippa took the piece of crumpled paper from Lucinda and read:

Dear Lucinda,

My uncle has been taken very ill and I won't be able to perform in the gala this evening as I'm going to the hospital now to be with him. Would you mind performing 'Life's a Dream' in my absence? You sang it so well the other day in rehearsal and at least the scouts will get to know of my songwriting ability, even if they can't hear me sing.

I hope you understand and are able to help.

Good luck.

Pippa x

Pippa couldn't hide her sorrow any longer and the tears started to fall, but she was in too deep to back out.

Lucinda ignored her. 'I'm just a bit worried they

won't let me change my song to yours at the last minute, unless you've officially asked me to.'

Pippa didn't even look up from the note. She felt as though she was signing her life away.

'Oh, Pippa, stop snivelling! Hurry and get cleaned up – we're going to be late. It'll all work out. I promise!' Lucinda said, with her fibbing fingers crossed behind her back.

Pippa ran off to the bathroom to sort out her blotchy face with some powder, and Lucinda made her way to English, grinning like the cat who'd got the cream.

11

Friday the Thirteenth

'I just can't face any more rehearsals,' said Molly, a slightly insane look on her face as she walked with Maria and Pippa to technology. 'For the first time in my life, I'm delighted to be going to sit at a computer to create spreadsheet formulae!'

Maria was thinking the opposite. She'd barely practised her piece for all the blogging and snooping she'd been doing. Still, thanks to her efforts, every student who'd written in asking *Yours, L'Etoilette* for help had been rescued. She must make proper use of the rehearsal time before lunch to give her own piano piece a good practice!

'You're quiet, Pips,' said Molly. 'You're just a bit

nervous, I expect. I can't wait to hear which one of your songs you've chosen. I love the fact you've kept it a secret from everyone. I haven't even heard all of them myself yet. Is it one of the ones that was on your web page?'

'No,' answered Pippa, trying to sound enthusiastic. 'It's actually the first song I ever wrote. No one except Uncle Harry's heard it yet.

Which wasn't strictly true, was it, Story-seeker? That should have read, no one except Uncle Harry and Lucifette.

You're right, I'm nervous anyway and the lyrics are kind of autobiographical, you know, about who I am, where I've come from and what my dreams are.'

'Oh how brilliant, Pippa. I can't wait to hear it! You're so lucky – bet you've not really needed to practise it at all, have you, if it's your own piece? What can they compare it to? It'll just come from the heart. You're so clever!' Molly said, proud of her gorgeous raven-haired friend. Pippa managed to beam through her guilt.

'What's the time, girls?' Lydia asked. 'This lesson is completely dragging. I've really got to get out of here

– my dad's dropping my cello back at ten thirty. Can you believe all four strings snapped yesterday? Talk about timing!'

'Still, better that it happened yesterday than tonight!' added Belle Brown from behind a monitor. 'It's ten o'clock.'

'Ten o'clock,' Pippa gasped. That hideous Lucinda would be on the phone to Miss Hart right now, giving the performance of a lifetime as Mrs Burrows. Pippa couldn't bear to think what was being said.

'So you understand, Miss Hart...' Lucinda was saying into her end of the phone, 'I simply can't leave Harry's side so will send a car to collect Pippa immediately. She would never forgive us if she wasn't there.'

'Of course, Mrs Burrows,' replied Miss Hart sympathetically. 'I can't imagine the shock and heartache you must all be going through. It is indeed a great shame, as you say, that Pippa won't be able to attend tonight's gala. The girls have all been working so hard. But there will be other chances next term. Some things are without doubt more important and should take priority. I will go myself and excuse Pippa from her lesson right away. Our thoughts at L'Etoile go out to you and your family. What time did you say the car would arrive?'

'Thank you, Miss Hart. You've been very kind. The driver will arrive at eleven o'clock. I've asked him to go to the private Garland entrance so as not to make a scene for Pippa. Could you possibly make sure she is there by eleven?'

'No problem at all, Mrs Burrows. Consider it done. Pippa will be with you shortly.' And with that, Miss Hart replaced the receiver, full of sorrow for poor Pippa, knowing what a horrible day lay ahead of her. She scanned the block of timetables on her office wall for 1 Alpha's schedule. There . . . technology . . . and off she went.

When Miss Hart appeared at the tech room doorway at ten minutes past ten, Pippa thought she might faint. Lucinda, who'd arrived mysteriously late for class, tried to catch her eye with a *don't-screw-this-up* look, but Pippa refused to glance in her direction. As Miss Hart approached, saying she needed a quiet word, Pippa could hear her heart beating in her chest. *Come on, Pippa! Pull yourself together – think record deal, think America, think superstar,* she said to herself, over and over again. It hadn't taken too much effort to be 'distraught', as per Lucinda's instructions. To be honest, distraught was the only emotion she did feel! The fact that Miss Hart was so kind and gentle, helping her to pack a bag for the journey, made it all much worse.

'There, there, Pippa,' said Miss Hart. 'Your Uncle Harry is going to be just fine. You mark my words. You're doing the right thing being with him and your mother. And nor should you worry about the gala. There will be so many opportunities for you to shine in the new year. You have such a raw, genuine talent, Pippa, I'm not at all worried about you missing your chance today and you shouldn't be either.'

The gala! The letter! Pippa had nearly forgotten. She ran over to Maria's desk and grabbed some paper and began writing the letter Lucinda could use as authorisation to sing 'Life's a Dream', should anyone query her change of song later on.

'What are you doing, Pippa?' Miss Hart asked in surprise.

Pippa stuffed the note into an envelope and handed it over. 'I've had an idea, Miss. Would you be kind enough to see that Lucifette, I mean, Lucinda Marciano, gets this, please?'

Miss Hart was bewildered but she took the letter

and promised to deliver it as soon as she could. She led Pippa down the back stairs to where her car was already waiting. 'Off you go, dear. You stay strong for your mother now. She needs you.' Pippa nodded and closed the car door.

And I need my mother, she thought. How had she allowed herself to get into such a mess?

12

How do You Solve a Problem Like Maria . . . and Molly?!

Maria was in a panic. Out of worry for Pippa and a desire to find out what was going on, she had immediately feigned a dizzy spell and the need to visit Nurse Payne. She had followed Miss Hart and Pippa down the corridor to the dorm, absorbing every snippet of their conversation, and then watched in despair as Pippa had been driven away in a very expensive-looking chauffeur-driven car.

What was going on? Poor Pippa! She had to get back to Molly and tell her what she'd seen.

Luckily, classes had finished for the day and the girls had been left to use the time before the gala commenced at six o'clock for rehearsal and general preening.

'What do you mean, she's gone?' Molly shrieked in alarm.

'Shhhh!' spluttered Maria. 'In here, quick.' She pulled Molly into one of the computer rooms.

'Gone where, FGS?' Molly asked.

'To visit her uncle in hospital, Miss Hart told her. But it just doesn't add up. That car – the one with the chauffeur that came to pick her up – was just . . .'

'Just what?!' Molly interrupted, exasperated with Maria for not being able to find the words.

'Just, er . . . well . . . too posh for Pippa's family. You know yourself Pippa said they don't have a lot of money. Why would Pippa's mum send a car like that? Anyway, surely her mum would have come to L'Etoile to break the news to Pippa herself. I know Mummy would do that if she had something horrible to tell us. It just doesn't make any sense.'

'I hardly think the car's a cause for concern, to be honest,' Molly scolded her sister, annoyed that she only ever considered the logistics of a situation – and suspiciously at that. 'I'm more worried about Pippa. I wish I was with her.'

Maria nodded. 'Why, oh why, has that girl not got a mobile yet? I told her it's only a matter of time before she gets caught with some emergency or another.'

'There's not a lot we can do about it now, is there? I suggest we go and speak to Miss Hart ourselves and find out if there's anything we can do to help,' Molly said.

'What good will that do? There's nothing we can do. Pippa's with her family and that's the best place for her at a time like this. I'd like to know more about that letter she asked Miss Hart to give Lucifette, though.'

'What letter — you never mentioned any letter!' Molly exploded.

'Didn't I? Oh, sorry. It's all been such a whirlwind. The letter Pippa scribbled in the dorm and asked Miss Hart to take to Lucifette before she left.'

'OK, now I definitely smell a rat! Pippa Burrows send Lucifette a letter? No chance! Now I'm convinced something's up!' Molly said, almost in tears herself.

'What did you just say, Moll?' Maria stopped her suddenly. 'Rat? Burrows . . . Rabbit . . . it's Pippa!' she sputtered. 'Pippa's the rabbit!'

'Slow down, Mimi,' Molly shook her sister by the arms, trying to calm her down. 'What are you talking about?!'

'The rabbit!' repeated Maria breathlessly. 'The

horrible email from this morning, the blinded rabbit in the headlights . . . it's . . . it's Pippa.'

Molly stopped in her tracks. But of course! It was a play on words – Pippa Burrows . . . Burrows – a rabbit burrows. How could they have missed it?

'Quick – get the email up again so we can have another look and see what else it'll tell us,' Molly said.

Maria was already on the computer, logging on to the haveyoursay@letoile.co.uk email account. Both girls waited impatiently for the mail to open.

To: haveyoursay@letoile.co.uk
From: email@starservice.com
Date: Wednesday 11th December – 7:04 a.m.

One little rabbit new to the scene
Met another who wanted to reign supreme
Like one in the headlights,
She'd follow her blind
What happened to that rabbit, we'll know in time.

They read the note again. It was so obvious now that they knew the little rabbit was Pippa. She was new to the scene, having won her scholarship to the school. And she'd gone off in a car – hence the headlights – but who was this person *'who thought she'd reign supreme'*? Would there be another email with more clues?

'Maria – there's got to be a way of finding out who sent this. Can't you do something?' Molly begged.

'There is a way of finding out who an email address is registered to, via the IP address – but I'm not sure I know how to do that kind of search. I've only ever seen it done once when Daddy had the IT guy over trying to find out who'd been sending those emails pretending to be him. Do you remember?'

Molly stood behind her sister at the screen and squeezed her shoulder in encouragement. If there was ever a good time for Maria to recall her techy expertise, it was now, and as she started tapping away, she opened up screen after screen of what Molly could only describe as gobbledygook.

'Ah ha!' Maria whooped. 'Here we are . . . email@ starservice.com is registered to . . .' She gasped in shock.

'Who, Mimi – who?!' Molly squealed.

'To Marciano Industries Ltd!' Maria blurted out.

Maria looked at Molly. Both girls were totally speechless. 'It's Lucifette! It just has to be. She must be using one of her father's email group addresses. Why, that over-confident, jumped-up little witch. How dare she think she can send a riddle we can't solve? And the bare-faced cheek of showing off like this.'

'But what does it all mean? What's Lucifette done with poor Pippa?' pleaded Molly. 'This whole thing is getting more awful by the minute!'

Maria paused for a moment and then started typing.

'What are you doing now?' asked Molly.

'I'm going to play Lucifette at her own game and email her back to say that unless she agrees to meet *Yours, L'Etoilette* in fifteen minutes in the Kodak Hall to explain herself, I'm going to post a blog right now exposing her to the whole school. Everyone's getting ready, so the hall will be dark and deserted – so at least we'll be able to see and confirm it's her before she sees us!' Maria hit send and sat back in her chair.

'What if she doesn't see the email in time and doesn't show?' moaned Molly, despondently.

'I don't even want to think about that, Moll. Come on – let's get there early so we can get a good view of the entrance.'

Ten minutes later, the twins were crouching under the lighting desk, which was on a raised platform at the back of the Kodak Hall. Luckily for them, there was a small tear in the black curtaining around the front of the desk, which gave them a great view of the whole auditorium. 'This had better work, Mimi!' Molly whispered.

'Shut up!' Maria shot back as she scoured the auditorium through the gap in the fabric. And then, 'Shhh – did you hear that? Someone's coming.'

Both girls held their breath as they heard footsteps tapping across the stage. And then a voice called out. '*Yours, L'Etoilette*? You here?'

Pushing Molly out of the way so she could get a better look, Maria saw the silhouette of Sally Sudbury standing in the middle of the stage.

'I don't believe it,' Maria breathed. 'What a coward! Lucifette can't even do her own dirty work – she's sent Sally to take the heat.'

'What are you going to do, Mimi? You can't talk to her – you'll totally blow your *Yours, L'Etoilette* cover.'

'Some things are just more important, Moll – like friends. Pippa's my friend and I'm going to help her, whatever the cost.'

With that, Maria ventured out from under the desk and called to Sally. 'Email@starservice? Is that you?'

Sally looked over in their direction, still unable to make out who exactly was talking to her. Maria made her way down the aisle to the stage and, as she did so, Sally's expression turned to one of relief.

'Maria!' Sally exclaimed. 'It's you!'

'And it's you, Sally Sudbury.' Maria responded coldly – not wanting to show that she was the least bit surprised at seeing Sally standing there. 'Too chicken to come out and explain things for herself, is she? Should have guessed.'

'I don't know what you mean, Maria,' Sally said timidly, and then it dawned on her that *Yours, L'Etoilette* had been bluffing when she had emailed saying she knew the identity of the email sender. 'Oh no!' Sally realised. 'You thought I was going to be Lucinda . . . I mean, that Lucinda was email@ starservice . . . I mean . . . oh dear, it's all getting very confusing. It was me . . . I sent that email.'

Molly burst out of the shadows behind Maria. 'Sally – I can't believe it. How . . . I mean . . . why did you send such an awful note about Pippa? We are right, aren't we . . . it is about Pippa, isn't it? What have you done with her?'

'Slow down, Molly!' Maria said calmly, starting to realise what might really be going on. 'Let Sally speak. Sally?'

'Oh, I'm so pleased it's you. I half-feared – well, I

won't tell you what I half-feared. I'm just so pleased it's you. It's all got so messy. Yes, Pippa is the rabbit. And I'm sorry if my email came across as threatening – I was just trying to be cryptic, in case it fell into the wrong hands. After all – you knew who *Yours, L'Etoilette* was, but I didn't! Could have been Lucinda for all I knew, then I would have been well and truly caught in the act! She'd kill me if she knew I was telling her secret!'

Maria smiled at her in encouragement. 'Never mind Lucifette, Sally. Now you know that I'm *Yours, L'Etoilette* – you do know I'm going to have to kill you, don't you?' And she laughed softly, immediately putting Sally at ease.

'Oh, Maria, Molly – it's so horrible. Lucinda's set a trap for Pippa, just to keep her from performing at tonight's gala.' Maria stood stiff, every muscle in her body frozen with fury.

'Sally, it's OK. Tell us exactly what's happened and maybe we can all try to fix it,' Molly said reassuringly.

'It's too late, it's too late . . .' Sally tailed off. She was sobbing. And, collapsing onto one of the theatre seats, she recounted the whole sordid, spiteful tale of the lies that Lucinda had spun to get Pippa out of the way so that she could sing Pippa's song as if it were her own handiwork.

'And that's not even the worst of it . . .' she sniffed. 'She managed to get Pippa to hand over one of her CDs which has both the backing track without a vocal on it to sing live to, and a full version with the vocal recorded live in the studio. She's not even planning to sing it herself – she's going to MIME!'

Molly and Maria recoiled in horror!

As Molly was stroking Sally's shoulder, which was bobbing up and down as she sobbed and sniffled, Maria was deep in thought about what to do to make all of this right. First things first, they had to get Pippa out of that blasted car, and back to L'Etoile.

'Sally,' Maria said. 'I need you to put all of your fear behind you for a minute and think clearly about how we can get a message to Pippa. You don't by some stroke of luck know who the driver is and have his number, do you?' Sally shook her head. 'It'll be one of Mr Marciano's company drivers. They're the only ones the family ever book.' Poor Sally really did look upset as she sat there hunched in her seat. But despite appearances, she was wracking her brains trying to come up with a way to help. Part of her couldn't believe she'd been brave enough to betray Lucinda. But she was glad she had.

'The only thing I do know about the drivers is that all the Marciano cars always fill up at one particular service station outside London because Mr Marciano owns it. They *always* stop there to top up – even if the tank's still half-full. We could try and work out what sort of time Pippa will be passing through there and get a message to her. Does that help?'

'Does that help? Are you kidding – well done, Sal!' Maria grabbed at the information she'd just been given as if it was the latest iPhone. Suddenly a plan began to develop in her head. It was a vague plan and it relied heavily on timing and luck, but it just might work.

'Moll, is Albie coming today with a delivery?' she asked.

'Yeah, it's Friday isn't it? He's coming at half-past one today. I can't wait.'

Molly turned to Sally. 'He's bringing those little grey suede pixie boots Kate Moss was wearing at the Brits – do you know the ones I mean?'

Sally looked vacant.

'Mollllllly! Not now. Have you got his number in your mobile?' Molly reached into her school bag and shook it like a box of tic-tacs at Maria. 'Right, call him,' Maria instructed, 'and then pass him to me!'

Molly hit speed-dial number 4. *What a saddo!* Maria thought, but quickly re-focused as Molly held out the phone to her. 'It's going straight to voicemail,' she sighed.

'You know what to do after the tone,' echoed Albie's voice . . . *Beeeeeeeep.*

Maria grabbed the handset. 'Albie? It's Molly and Maria Fitzfoster here on Molly's phone. We need to speak with you urgently – it could be a matter of life and death.' Maria hung up and looked at her watch. If the car had left L'Etoile just after eleven, by her calculations, they should be hitting the service station by about twelve-thirty. Eeeek, they had forty-five minutes to locate Albie and convince him to go and pick up Pippa on his bike. They just had to hope he was in the shower or something and that he hadn't left home yet – he'd never pick up his mobile if he was driving.

All three girls looked at each other. They felt as though a tornado had just swept through their lives – leaving a trail of destruction and uncertainty in its wake.

'I want to thank you, Sally,' Molly began. 'I can't

begin to imagine why you decided to snitch on Lucifette and save Pippa, but I'm glad you did.'

'Yeah, thanks Sal,' echoed Maria. 'Can't have been easy making a move against Lucifette. She's pretty much got you where she wants you, hasn't she?'

'You've no idea,' Sally volunteered. 'How can I ever be seen to be going against her? She'll have me and Mum out on the street quicker than you can say Coco Chanel!' Sally looked so vulnerable sitting there with her knees curled up in her enormous baggy jumper. 'I'm not sure how I'm going to get away with this one. We'll have to come up with something, girls . . . Please, I'll need your help to cover this up; she must never know it was me!'

'Don't worry, Sal,' Maria answered, impressed by the way Sally had conducted herself. 'When it all comes out in the wash, we'll make out that Pippa caved in and phoned us from the car – and as for the whole M-I-M-E situation – well, I, in my total brilliance, could have discovered that, couldn't I?' Sally knew it was inappropriate, but she suddenly felt an overwhelming wave of happiness wash over her.

'Talking about the MIME situation – what on earth are we going to do about the gala situation?' Sally asked, looking panicky again.

'Don't worry about that,' answered Maria confidently. 'Moll and I will think of something. For the minute, we just need to get Pippa back.'

Bbbbrrrriiiinnnng . . . bbbbrrrrriiiiinnnng . . . Molly's phone sang out. 'Albie?' she asked desperately. 'Oh, thank goodness. I'll just pass you to Maria.'

In no time at all, Maria had revealed the whole sorry story to Albie, who felt very protective towards the girls he delivered expensive clothes to every Friday afternoon. It was his favourite job of the week and he was more than happy to be part of a rescue operation for them. Even before the phone call had finished, he'd grabbed a spare helmet for Pippa and was outside his flat revving his motorbike.

'Call me when you've got her, Albie. And thanks!'

It was far too risky for Sally to be caught hanging out with the twins by Lucinda, so the new trio made arrangements to meet again at twelve-forty-five, well away from the Kodak Hall, which was beginning to become the focus for most of the school. The gala was due to start at six o'clock, so with only a few hours to go, everyone was frantic.

Molly and Maria could hear Faye shrieking.

'Who's got Daisy's skirt? What? Oh FGS, Alice! It's coral tie-dye with a pearl and feather motif . . . Oh

'FGS, Lara – not you as well . . . does that look like it belongs to you? Get it off or you'll split it!'

Molly laughed. 'Who'd be Faye right now? Not me!'

Maria humoured her sister with a giggle but was too concerned with Operation Pippa to respond further.

As soon as the twins were alone in their dorm again, Maria was logging on to the haveyoursay@letoile. co.uk email account.

'What are you doing now?' Molly muttered.

'I've just emailed Sally for Mr Marciano's assistant's number – there's one thing we haven't taken into consideration. How we are going to get Pippa away from the driver? If a biker swoops in and grabs Pippa, the driver's sure to call the police and say she's been kidnapped. Somehow we need to get a message to the driver that it's OK for his passenger to go with Albie.'

Ping. Sally's emailed response flashed up on the screen.

'Ah, here we go. Molly, will you ring his secretary and pretend to be Lucifette? It's our only hope. If you're really rude and obnoxious she'll believe you're her. Just tell her that the idiot driver picked up the wrong passenger and that you've arranged yourself for a taxi bike to collect Pippa from the service station and bring her back to L'Etoile. That way we're also guaranteed that the driver will stop at the services. Just hope he doesn't get the message too early, tell Pippa and panic her. She won't know what is going on!'

Molly took a deep breath and made the call to the long-suffering Elodie Wyatt. It was easy.

'Wowsers, that poor assistant. She didn't even bat an eyelid that I wasn't Lucifette. She must have had her wits scared right out of her. She was like one of those nodding dogs that sit on car shelves – all, "Yes sir, yes madam" with no mind of her own,' Molly said as she hung up. 'So what now?'

'So now we wait,' Maria announced calmly.

'So now we get thinking!' Molly protested. 'We're only halfway there, Mimi. How are we going to expose Lucifette's miming exploits during her performance?'

'Elementary, my dear Molly,' taunted Maria annoyingly.

'Oh, don't tell me, you've already thought of that too!' grinned Molly with mischief in her eyes. 'Do tell . . .'

13

The Great Escape

$\mathcal{I}$n the back of the huge, chauffeur-driven car, Pippa was full of regret. She didn't care about the stupid record company audition. If only she could turn back the clock and tell that ghastly Lucinda what she thought of her, she'd do it in a heartbeat. She had betrayed herself and, in turn, her family and her friends. Oh, her friends. How could she have been so deceitful to Molly and Maria when they'd gone out of their way to be so kind to her?

Just as they pulled up at a service station, the driver's mobile rang.

Albie, meanwhile, was astride his motorbike, eyes glued to every vehicle entering the petrol station. He was half-terrified he might have already missed Pippa – so you can imagine how relieved he felt when he spied the gleaming black Cadillac cruising onto the forecourt.

You might wonder, Story-seeker, how he knew it was the correct car? Maria had taken down the registration number of course when she'd seen Pippa get in and drive away that morning. Told you she was methodical, didn't we?

As soon as he saw the car arrive, he walked over, being sure to remove his helmet so as not to scare her, and tapped on the window. He'd only met her a couple of times at the school with Molly when he'd dropped off her orders, so he was praying she'd recognise him!

'Albie?' Pippa exclaimed with glee when she clapped eyes on him. She was out of the car in a split second, so relieved to see a friendly face. She could have thrown her arms around him but decided that might be a bit much. 'What are you doing here?'

Albie grinned. 'Pippa – the twins sent me. You've been stitched up. You've got to come back to the school with me – they'll explain everything then. It was Lucinda . . .'

'I bloomin' knew it!' Pippa cried. 'But what about the driver – he'll think I've been kidnapped if I don't get back in the car.'

'Don't worry about that.' Albie grinned again. 'The twins have sorted it. Molly cancelled the car by pretending to be Lucinda. She told 'em there'd been a mistake and you'd be getting a taxi bike back to L'Etoile.' As he explained, he waved over at the driver and gave a thumbs-up. 'Wave and smile then, Pippa!' he commanded, helping her to fasten her helmet. Pippa waved and grinned like a mad woman at the driver, who nodded and pulled away.

It was a relatively short journey back to L'Etoile. Motorbikes were so much quicker than cars, weaving in and out of the traffic. Pippa did feel a bit guilty about one thing, though – and decided there and then that she'd omit this part of the story if she ever relayed it to her grandchildren – or her mother, for that matter, who'd have killed her daughter for ever riding on the back of a motorbike!

Molly, Maria and Sally were beside themselves with anticipation. Twelve forty-five had come and gone and they'd had no text or phone call from Albie as to whether he'd managed to intercept the car successfully and grab Pippa. Albie would later be mortified about this, as he had remembered to write a text just before they set off, saying, 'Got her!', but in his haste had forgotten to press send. By one o'clock, the girls couldn't wait in their room any longer and decided it would be best to go and hide themselves behind one of the caretaker's sheds at the rear entrance to Garland where they usually waited for Albie and his fashion deliveries. By their meticulous calculations, Maria and Sally had estimated that, with the speed of motorbike travel, if all had gone to plan, Pippa should be coming down the drive by about one-fifteen . . . and, of course, they'd been spot-on!

'There she is!' shrieked Molly and all three girls sprinted towards Pippa, who was already in floods of tears. Albie and Pippa had thought it best to leave the bike hidden in the bushes halfway up the drive and walk the rest of the way so as not to alert anyone that they were there with the sound of the engine.

'Oh, girls!' Pippa gasped. 'How did you unravel all of this? How can I ever thank you? Maria, you're so clever – I bet you hatched this whole thing.' Pippa stopped short when she noticed Sally Sudbury hanging back behind the twins, trying to make herself look as small as humanly possible.

'It's OK, Pips,' Maria said quickly. 'She's with us. If it hadn't been for her spilling the beans about Lucifette's evil plan, we'd never have known it was happening.'

Pippa, whose trusting nature had taken a bit of a battering of late, looked suspiciously at Sally, and then smiled. *Oh well, just this last time,* she thought to herself and gave Sally a big hug too.

'Albie, you're a complete star,' said Molly as she flung her arms around a very red-faced, but happy, Albie. 'Wait till we're home in London this Christmas. We're going to throw you the best party you've ever had!' Albie was now almost purple-faced below his curly red hair.

'Come on, Pippa, and we'll explain the whole thing on the way. You won't believe some of it! It's so good to have you back.' Maria squeezed Pippa's hand affectionately.

'I'd better see you later, girls,' Sally beamed at her new friends. 'The fewer opportunities Lucifette has to bust us together, the better. Pippa, you HAVE to find somewhere to hide and quickly.'

'Wait a minute, Sal – did you just call her Lucifette?' Maria asked. 'Amazing.'

'Loving your work, Sal!' echoed Molly. 'See you at the gala for part deux of the big Lucifette exposé!'

'Mimi, was this really the best place you could come up with?' asked Molly, nearly gagging at the smell of bird poo.

'Well, if you've got any better ideas – I'm all ears!' snapped Maria. 'There's a workbench for a dressing-table, and a plug for your straighteners – what more do you need, FGS?'

When Maria had racked her brains earlier that morning for a safe place to hide Pippa and for them all to get ready for the gala, the lake boathouse had seemed like the obvious place. It was near enough to the Kodak Hall for them to sneak back and forth unseen and had its own outdoor loo, running water and electricity.

Molly was not-so-secretly horrified at the environment she had to work with, but the thought of Lucinda's face when she realised she'd been rumbled was keeping her sane.

As Molly busied herself setting up the makeshift dressing room, Pippa just kept firing questions at the twins, trying to work out how the day's events had unfolded. The biggest shocker for all of them had been the bravery of lovely Sally.

'Oh, Sally was absolutely fabulous,' Molly marvelled.

'If not a little ingenious,' Maria joined in. 'The way she sent me that anonymous email to the *Yours, L'Etoilette* address.'

Pippa was a bit confused. 'What do you mean, sent you the email? If she sent it to *Yours, L'Etoilette*, how did it find its way to you? Actually, if it was anonymous, how did you even find out it was from her?'

Maria looked at Molly and Molly looked back at Maria – both in shock at the ease with which Maria had quite forgotten her anonymity as the mysterious *Yours, L'Etoilette*.

'Oh, Pippa, I reckon it's going to take weeks of midnight feast chats for us to fully explain all this to you. But for starters – and if you tell another living soul, you're dead – I'm *Yours, L'Etoilette!*' Maria said.

Pippa smiled in admiration. 'You're so clever, Maria – although I should have guessed really. Who else in this school would have the know-how and techy expertise to pull off something like that around a jam-packed timetable!'

Maria glowed at Pippa's compliment. 'Oh, it's been soooo difficult keeping it from you, Pips,' Molly cried out in relief. 'The only chance Mimi has to check and update it away from prying eyes is in the mornings before school, so you did us a big favour every time you left the dorm early for your meetings and rehearsals.'

'Moll, I was only leaving early to either rendezvous with stupid Lucifette who kept sneaking me notes to arrange follow-up meetings, or I was just trying to leave early to avoid bumping into her altogether! I felt so awful deceiving you both. All I really wanted was for you two to rumble me by asking too many questions – but now I see you were both too busy with your own sneaky business to notice any weird behaviour!' The trio looked at each other fondly and burst out laughing.

'We've been so stupid, haven't we?' admitted Molly. 'Let's make a pact – no more secrets?'

'No more secrets!' Maria and Pippa sang back in unison and the three girls piled their hands one on top of the other to seal the deal.

'Talking about secrets . . . Come on, Maria, spill the beans on how we're going to expose Lucifette tonight then,' Molly urged, desperate to hear her sister's clever plans.

'Well,' Maria started as she drew the girls close. 'It involves you, Pippa, a spare radio microphone and a well-timed CD swap.'

14

The Calm Before the Storm

*F*ive o'clock approached, and seemed to mark the start of the gala audience arrivals.

As one fabulous car after another rolled up the drive, the spectacle of outfits and hairdos was enough to keep *Hiya!* magazine in print for years to come. The guest list read like a *Who's Who* of the entertainment industry.

Leading the throng of parents and industry folk to the theatre was, of course, Madame Ruby – in all her glory. She was sporting the most dazzling gold sequinned gown and a hairdo to rival Marge Simpson. Parents cooed and aahed as she recounted tales of their daughters' achievements over the course of the term.

Mr and Mrs Marciano, however, were absolutely nowhere to be seen, which was starting to send Madame Ruby into a pink mist.

'Helen,' she squawked. 'Have you phoned Elodie Wyatt?'

Poor Miss Hart, who hadn't even had time to change, what with overseeing the girls all afternoon, was scuttling after the Grand Madame with yet another clipboard stuffed with notes.

'I've just spoken to her, Ruby – for the fourth time since lunch – and she assures me that they are en route.'

'En route . . . en route . . . that could mean anyth—' Madame Ruby was stopped in her ranting tracks by a very large man in a dinner suit, waddling down the path sporting what could only have been magnifying-glass spectacles.

'Calamity, darling!' Madame exclaimed, displaying every one of her lipstick-coated teeth. 'How are you? Welcome to L'Etoile. Thank you so much for coming. The girls are simply dying to meet you.'

The man in question, Calamity Mossback, was one of America's hottest talent scouts, and had come all the way over from Creative Management Inc. in Los Angeles. He held out a stubby-fingered hand to Madame Ruby.

'The pleasure is all mine, Ruby, dear. Now let me at 'em. What time does this shindig start anyway? I've come straight from the airport and I'm on the red-eye back to LA tonight.'

'Six o'clock sharp,' Madame Ruby stated confidently. 'It'll be worth the wait, dear man. I can assure you I have some real diamond talent in this new crop of starlets. Look out for Lucinda Marciano – she's my hot tip for you – you will know her mother and father, of course.'

Calamity's hairy ears pricked up. 'Marciano, eh? I'd best get the best seat in the house then, hadn't I?' He grabbed a glass of champagne from a passing waiter, and continued down the path to the Kodak Hall – completely oblivious to having toppled the entire tray in his wake.

As the cars continued to empty out their glamorous occupants, the buzz around the dorms was at fever pitch. The only girl who was calm for the first time in three weeks was Faye, who had now successfully dressed each and every starlet to perfection. She was just doing a last-minute costume check and felt really proud of herself.

'We just love them, Faye!' Sofia and Charlotte called out as she whizzed past. 'They're the most beautiful opera costumes we've ever seen.'

Lucinda, one had to admit, looked stunning in a red 'look at me' chiffon number which her mother had indeed sent over from Paris. Having seen rather less of Sally than she would have liked that day, Lucinda was in dire need of some attention and had decided to use the Garland corridor as a catwalk to see how many gasps of admiration she could amass from her classmates at the sight of her in her glorious dress. But apparently everyone had lost their voice! Not a single girl uttered a word to her. *How dare they?* she thought, turning the same colour as her dress. But even Lucinda wouldn't stoop so low as to fish for a compliment. 'SAAAAALLLLLLLY!' she screeched into thin air.

Where was she? She couldn't be still rehearsing that same idiotic poem. Didn't she realise she was going to totally bomb, no matter how much practice she put in? 'SAAAAAAAALLLLLLLLLLLLLLLYYYYYYY,' she called so loudly that her voice cracked.

Sally appeared suddenly from the Garland ladies room, where, if the truth be known, she'd been hiding for most of the afternoon. Not that she'd really needed to; it was just that she was terrified Lucinda would see into her soul and discover how she'd betrayed her to Pippa and the twins. It wasn't that she regretted her decision to do the right thing for once – not for one second – it had felt wonderful to do some good for a change and to be on the receiving end of a hug. She just felt she couldn't face Lucinda . . . not yet . . . not until it was almost over.

'Where the heck have you been? I've told you a hundred times, there's no point practising that stupid poem. Let's go – I want to see if Mom and Pop have arrived. I'm quite surprised no one's come to escort us down, to be honest.' Sally, as usual, maintained a submissive silence, but was relieved that Lucinda seemed even more self-obsessed than usual.

'Oh, never mind – come on,' said Lucinda and dragged Sally, still clutching her poem, to the Kodak Hall.

Beep, beep. Maria snatched up her mobile from the makeshift make-up table.

'Yikes, it's Mum and Dad. They're here and want to see us before the show,' she announced to Molly, who was putting the final touches to Pippa's hair and make-up.

'What time is it?' Molly looked up.

'Nearly half-five,' answered Maria. 'Are you almost done?'

'Just give me two secs and I'll be with you.' Molly

grabbed the enormous – now nearly empty – can of hairspray, and released a last fog of spray onto Pippa's beautiful 'up-do'.

'There!' Molly gasped, as Pippa stood up quickly and ran into an area of the boathouse where she could breathe without swallowing a mouthful of hairspray.

The three girls looked at each other in awe.

'We look amazing!' said Molly, ecstatic. In addition to the stunning hair and make-up she'd managed to produce in an hour of madness, Molly had added her own accessories to the gorgeous outfits Faye had provided for all three of them – and had to admit she'd outdone herself. Luckily, Pippa had left her dress in the dorm before she had been forced to pull out of the gala that morning.

'How do you feel, Pippa?' Molly asked, holding up a rather small mirror in her direction. Pippa, desperately trying not to well up and smudge her carefully applied mascara, swirled around, admiring her appearance. She hardly recognised herself.

'Oh, Moll, you're a genius,' she exclaimed. 'I feel a million dollars. Lucifette won't know what to be more angry about – the fact that I'm going to scupper her evil plan, or the fact that I look like a real star!'

'Yes, well done – you've done a fabulous number

on us,' confirmed Maria. 'But we'd best be going. We have to at least say hi to Mum and Dad before we go on or they'll be devastated – and you're up to perform second, Molly, so we need to get a move on!'

'Second? How could I have forgotten? I've got butterflies now!' Molly grabbed her script from the side. 'Please don't let me forget my words, please don't let me forget my words,' she muttered to herself, looking to the sky for help.

Pippa grabbed Molly's hand. 'You'll be wonderful – just wait till they get a load of *Molly Hollywood*!' Molly's blue eyes twinkled back at her.

'You go on, both of you,' Pippa continued. 'My legs are like jelly. I could do with a couple of minutes alone to run through my song anyway and you're both on well before Lucifette – *and me*! I can't believe she managed to get the headline spot as the last act of the evening. She really doesn't miss a trick, does she?'

'Well, all the better for you to be the Grand Finale no one knows they're going to get!' said Maria with a glint in her eye.

'Break a leg.' Maria hugged Pippa. 'And don't you worry about a thing. I'll be ready for you. Remember – when you hear Sofia and Charlotte singing their "Flower Duet" – and you'll definitely hear that –

scoot round to the back of the hall by the sound and lighting desk. There's a big black curtain running from the raised desk platform down to the floor to hide the scaffold, so there will be plenty of space for you to hide there with us until the penultimate act has finished and Lucifette has been introduced.'

'Who is on before Lucifette?' asked Pippa.

'Poor Sally,' announced Maria. 'No doubt she'll be a nervous wreck by then, after everything that's happened today.' Molly and Pippa winced in sympathy.

'Are you sure you'll be able to switch my vocal track that Lucifette is planning to mime to to my purely instrumental track?'

'Don't worry!' Maria said. 'Moll and I will think of something. Have we ever let you down?'

Pippa gave the twins one last squeeze. 'Love you, girls,' she breathed. 'Thank you.'

And with one last sweep of lip gloss, Molly grabbed Maria and crept out of the boathouse, closing the door firmly behind them.

'Please let this work,' pleaded Pippa quietly to herself. 'I promise I'll never screw up again.'

15

A Star-Studded Christmas Gala

*T*he twins entered the main hall just in time to see Madame Ruby link arms with their poor, unsuspecting father and lead him and their mum, who had been left somewhat behind, over to two empty seats.

'There they are, Mimi!' Molly cried, her heart jumping. 'Yeah, and look who old Ruby's putting them next to!' Maria gulped.

'Mr and Mrs Fitzfoster, I'd like you to meet some of my other VVIP guests – Blue and Serafina Marciano.' Madame Ruby snaked around both couples. She couldn't have been more delighted with her introduction and hoped the whole theatre was watching in awe.

Mrs Marciano held out a diamond-laden hand to Mr Fitzfoster.

'Brian, darling – I can hardly believe we've never met before. All of the Marciano diamonds are Fitzfoster diamonds,' she sang, wiggling her fingers in his face to show off her jewels.

'Mrs Marciano, Mr Marciano. I know you by reputation, of course,' Mr Fiztfoster said. He was too polite to allow his face to show anything other than a smile.

'This is my wife, Linda.' The glamorous Mrs Fitzfoster stepped forward to say hello. Even Blue Marciano's breath was taken away by her beauty – which earned him a well-aimed ankle kick from his wife's sharp stiletto heels.

'Mummy! Daddy!' Molly and Maria shrilled as they launched themselves at their parents – who had never been so grateful to be interrupted by their daughters.

'Darlings . . . let me look at you both – gosh, you've grown up so much! Daddy and I have missed your cheeky faces!' Mrs Fitzfoster enveloped both the girls in the biggest cuddle she could muster. 'Don't you both look divine! Good job, Moll!' Linda said proudly.

'Mimi, I'm so proud of you for letting your sister at

you with the curling tongs. Didn't think you had it in you!' mocked Mr Fitzfoster gently, looking at his girls lovingly.

Maria thought at that moment how awful it must be for Pippa to be doing all of this alone tonight without her mother being there. But the diary clash with her own school had meant that Mrs Burrows would never have been able to make it. Maria, however, hadn't let that get in her way and had, of course, come up with a plan.

'Daddy – did you bring the camera like I asked?'

'Would I dare disobey either of my daughters?' Brian Fitzfoster said and flashed her a glimpse of the newest, state-of-the-art video camera.

'Great – be sure to get Moll and me, obviously, but would you also film the last two acts too? They're on the programme. I, er . . . need the footage for a gift.' Mr Fitzfoster looked suspicious but agreed.

'Thanks – wish us luck!' the twins cried out.

'My Lords, Ladies and Gentlemen,' came Madame Ruby's voice over the microphone, a single spotlight picking her out against the rich, red-velvet safety curtain. 'Welcome, one and all, to L'Etoile, School for Stars. I give you this year's Christmas gala . . .'

And as the orchestra struck up the tune 'There's

No Business Like Show Business', the audience erupted into applause.

'Molly, Maria! Are you trying to give me a heart attack?' gasped Miss Hart. 'I've had staff members looking absolutely everywhere for you. Where on earth have you been?' she asked, exasperated. 'Don't answer that!' she continued. 'Molly, stay here as you're on in about seven minutes, and Maria, go to the dressing rooms and stay there until you're called. No wandering off. Am I making myself clear?'

Neither twin dared argue and simply hugged each other for luck. They'd been through enough nannies to recognise a woman on the edge! Molly stood at the side of the stage, trying desperately to run through her lines in her head.

'Five ... six ... seven ... eight!' Molly swung round to see a petrified Heavenly Smith marking out her dance routine in the wings.

'Don't worry!' Molly said in a stage whisper.

'It's too late now! Wish me luck!' Heavenly said as Madame Ruby announced her name.

'Ladies and Gentlemen, I give you Miss Heavenly Smith.'

And with a shove from Miss Hart, Heavenly leapt through the curtain to give the performance of her life.

Molly's words were starting to make her feel nauseous. She could see acts three, four and five (Betsy, Nancy and Elizabeth) lining up by the door waiting to follow her on. Trying to get a grip of her nerves, she thought about Pippa and what she must be going through all alone in that boathouse, dreading what might go wrong with the big plan. 'Oh, it'll be fine,' she scolded herself. 'It'll have to be!'

Explosive applause erupted again and a grinning Heavenly flitted past her. 'Break a leg, Molly! You'll love it out there!!'

Molly could hear Madame Ruby describing her act. 'And our next artist is a divine little actress by the name of Molly Fitzfoster. Molly will be performing a split personality piece for you. See how she jumps from persona to persona as if the previous one never existed. Ladies and Gentlemen . . . I give you Miss Molly Fitzfoster!'

And, with a heaving chest, Molly grabbed her chair and glided out, all smiles and confidence, into the spotlight.

Her effortless performance was met with laughter and booming applause as she took a bow. As she ran off stage, she crashed straight into Maria.

'Oh, Mimi! What are you doing here – I thought you weren't allowed to stay and watch, seeing as you're on nearer the end!'

'Would I miss your big moment?' Maria announced. 'I swapped with Betsy, who was up next, so I could see you. You were amazing! Good job, Moll.'

'Thanks so much. And this means I'll get to watch you too.' Miss Hart shot the girls a warning look to be quiet.

'So next for your delectation, Ladies and Gentlemen, I give you an exquisite pianist by the name of Bets . . .' Madame Ruby frowned as she attempted to read through the crossings-out and new scribble on her script. 'Ah, another Fitzfoster . . . of equal brilliance, we hope . . . Maria Fitzfoster.'

Maria strode confidently over to the huge, black, grand piano, which stood on a built-out part of the staging. As she sat down, she composed herself for a moment and then launched into the most exquisite piano performance you could imagine. The audience were once again on their feet in raptures as Maria took a bow and exited the stage.

'Oh, Mimi – you were divine!' said Molly, who had managed to get Miss Hart to allow her to stay on to hear her sister's act.

'Really? Thanks, Moll – felt a bit of pressure there for a minute having to follow your triumph! Cheers for that, BTW!'

Molly threw her arms around Maria and whispered, 'Right – that's us done and dusted – now on to Pippa! Let's get this show on the road!'

16

Lucifette Gets Her Comeuppance

The dressing room was a war zone. Lucinda was sitting at the main make-up chair with one of the glamsquad, pretending to rehearse her song. Sally was cowering in a corner clenching her fists in an attempt to stop her hands from shaking. Sofia and Charlotte were singing like a couple of canaries in their matching yellow dresses. Alice Parry was at another mirror adjusting the silk flowers in her *My Fair Lady* hat, moaning that she was losing her voice. And between Daisy, desperately trying to tune her bassoon, and Lydia doing the same with her cello, it was like opening night at *The Royal Variety Performance*.

Molly and Maria were hunting through the dressing-room debris like commandos trying their hardest not to be seen. 'Where did you say you put it?' Molly hissed, incredulous that her genius of a sister could mess up something so important at this point.

'It was on the chair by the make-up mirror with the rest of my stuff,' Maria groaned. 'Someone must have moved it all. Oh no – it's sitting under that tissue box by Lucifette! Of all the luck!'

Molly looked at Maria in complete disbelief.

'I couldn't help it!' blurted out Maria. 'I left in such a hurry when I thought I was going to miss your performance that I didn't even think. How was I to know Lucifette would pick that seat?'

Suddenly Molly realised Sally was trying to catch their eye.

'What's up?' Sally mouthed.

'PIP-PA'S C-D!' Molly mouthed back and signalled to where Lucinda was sitting. Sally glanced across and spotted a silver CD poking out from underneath a tissue box.

Sally rolled her eyes, then jumped up and walked over to the mirror.

'L-L-Lucinda?' she stammered. Lucinda flashed her a look that would kill.

'What?' she snapped.

'Er, I just wondered if there was any hairspray I could borrow . . .' And with that, Sally leaned across Lucinda, sending the whole make-up table – including the tissue box – flying.

'SAAAAALLLLLYYYYYYY – you imbecile. Get out of my sight! NOW!' Lucinda screamed at her.

'I'm sorry, so sorry, sorry everyone . . .' As Sally bent to pick up the blusher brushes and lip glosses she caught the CD case under her foot and shot it backwards in the twins' direction. No one noticed a thing. Sally winked at the twins and continued Operation Clear-up. Molly blew her a kiss and they exited.

'That girl deserves a medal!' exclaimed Molly once they were safely out of earshot. 'Imagine the sort of onslaught she's experiencing at the hands of Lucifette now!'

'I know – she's a total honey,' agreed Maria. 'Blimey, Molly, time's getting on – they've probably gone through about ten more acts since we left the stage. We've got to get to the sound desk and get this CD swapped with the one with Pippa's voice on it. This will only work if we can replace it with this clean backing track.'

'You don't have to tell me!' protested Molly. 'I'm in on this already – remember?'

'I'm sorry – just nerves, I guess. There's just so much at stake!' Maria answered.

The angelic voices of Sofia and Charlotte echoed around the theatre. 'There's only this one and then Sally to go! Sound desk – now!'

Molly followed Maria through the foyer and into the back of the theatre. No one noticed them sneak in as everyone was facing the stage, totally mesmerised by the performance. As they climbed the small staircase to the raised platform where Mr Potts was sitting at the sound desk, Molly felt a tug at her dress.

'Pippa!' she exclaimed. Pippa motioned to her to shhhhh and disappeared beneath the curtain below them.

'What are you girls doing here?' Mr Potts fretted as he tried to remain focused on the stage.

'Sorry, Mr Potts,' Maria smiled brightly. 'I'm just so interested to see how this all works. You really are a marvel, the way you've held this whole show together. The sound is just tremendous . . . I don't know anyone who could have done a better job . . . truly!'

'Thank you, Maria,' Mr Potts said. 'I suppose it wouldn't hurt for you to stay for just a moment.'

Ha! Flattery will get you everywhere, Maria thought.

'Could I help you at all? There are only a couple of acts to go and I'd love to be able to tell my parents I'd actually helped with the technical side of the show as well as performing.'

Mr Potts looked at Maria, slightly bemused. This young lady really was quite different from the rest of the starlets. None of them had ever shown any interest in the nuts and bolts of production. Besides, there were only two acts left to go and only one needed technical help – the final act.

'Grab that folder of CDs over there. In the compartment numbered nineteen, there is one entitled Lucinda Marciano, "Life's a Dream". Pass it to me, would you, and give it a wipe on the cloth there.'

Maria couldn't believe her luck. As she grabbed the CD file and fingered through the pages she spotted number nineteen. She reached her hand down to where Molly was crouching, ready and waiting with the replacement CD. In a swift movement, hidden by the polishing cloth, Maria completed the swap and Molly ducked under the curtain to join Pippa, who was sitting there shaking with nerves.

'All done!' Molly whispered excitedly. Pippa was white.

'Oh Pippa, don't be scared – just think about Lucifette's face when you waltz up that centre aisle belting out for real the song she's pretending to sing.' Pippa turned even more ashen. Molly squeezed her hand as they heard Sally being announced on stage, reciting her 'Recipe for Perfect Friendship' poem, which she'd written herself. Sort of written herself . . . she'd taken a famous reading she'd once heard at a wedding, 'Recipe for the Perfect Wedding Cake,' and put her own slant on it.

As the audience applauded her entrance, Pippa grabbed Molly's arm. 'Where's the microphone?' she spluttered in a panic.

'Here it is!' declared Maria as she popped her head through the split in the curtain. 'I even got old Potts to show me how to put a new, full battery in. Not taking any chances now we've come this far!'

Pippa smiled and grabbed it. She suddenly felt so much better with her friends at her side. All three girls stopped to listen to Sally's poetry recital. To their delight, Sally was actually doing rather well. Her poem was simple, beautiful – and clever. She was coming to the end:

Take 4 tablespoons of love
A cup of loyalty
Six grams of fun and laughter,
A pinch of luck and a kilo of adventure.
Mix until well blended
And bake gently forever.

The audience exploded into applause – there were even a few whoops of appreciation.

'Oh, I'm sooooo pleased for her,' Molly hugged her knees to her chest. 'She's such a good writer, isn't she?' Pippa and Maria nodded in agreement.

'Well, my goodness me. Thank you, Sally Sudbury,' said Madame Ruby, slightly surprising herself. 'And now to our final performance of the evening. A singer with whom you are more than familiar, by the name of Lucinda Marciano.' As she mentioned Lucinda's name, she couldn't help throwing Blue Marciano a little wave from the stage. 'Lucinda will be performing "Life's a Dream", which will seem all the more exciting to you all when I tell you that this talented young lady penned this song herself!' The audience gasped.

'What the . . . ?' gasped Pippa. 'How dare she! That evil little . . .'

♥ *160* ♥

'Don't, Pippa! Not now – not when you're so close. You need to channel your energy into your performance. She'll get her comeuppance and it's moments away.'

Pippa lowered her eyes and, as she did so, Molly whipped out her lip gloss and held Pippa's chin up. With one swift stroke, Pippa was transformed into a goddess again. 'Go get 'em, tiger!' Molly said, and Pippa stepped into the shadows at the back of the hall.

As she heard the melody of her song, her very first song, float out across the theatre, all her fears fell away. She watched Lucinda walk onto the stage in the distance and raise the microphone to her mouth to begin. Pippa, unknown to anyone, least of all Lucinda, began to sing too. She sang out of the darkness at the back of the hall; Lucinda's lips synched to her voice in perfect unison.

Molly and Maria, who had also emerged from their hiding place, were in awe of what they were witnessing. It couldn't have been more perfectly executed.

Pippa's incredible vocal range and tone filled every nook, every cranny and every heart in the theatre as she slowly began to glide from the shadows. Her silver gown shimmered like a minnow darting through a stream as the lights picked her out. Only those in the back row of the auditorium had started to murmur, unsure whether this was part of the show or not.

If you look into my eyes
You'll see a shining light

More and more of the audience turned round but Lucinda was too engrossed in her own performance and her own shining light to notice.

Pippa continued to glide through the central aisle, looking like a mermaid emerging from the depths of the sea.

Of everything within I hid from sight
Nothing is what it seems

Suddenly Lucinda, still miming away, was aware of whispering below her. At first, and unable to see clearly into the theatre beyond her parents in the front row, she presumed the gasps and whispers were due to her captivating the audience. She continued to mouth the words . . .

So use the love and keep the faith,
And you'll find that life's a dream

. . . but before she reached the end of the final lyric, her mouth fell open in utter surprise. Pippa had reached the stage and was making her way up the steps towards her, like a silver goddess riding the crest of a wave.

Now, Story-seeker, at the risk of annoying you by interrupting at such a crucial moment, we're going to give you a couple of guesses as to what happened next. Can you guess? No? Then we'll continue.

As Pippa belted out the final few notes of her beautiful song, turning to face the delighted audience, Lucinda ran off the stage like the little coward we all knew she was.

Pippa stood tall and proud, bathing in the spotlight and applause. People were stamping their feet on the floor, whooping, whistling, clapping . . . and that was just the parents! The rest of her year had all been standing at the back of the theatre to watch Lucinda's 'performance of the night' and so had all been there, watching open-mouthed.

Madame Ruby was aghast and furious at what had just occurred on her stage, but couldn't do anything other than congratulate Pippa and draw the gala to a close.

'Hey, Ruby!' Calamity Mossback rasped as Madame Ruby made her way down to her guests. 'Who was the girl in the silver? She's got it! Send me her details in the morning. Oh, and the blonde actress. What a looker and what a talent! I wanna talk to them both.'

Madame Ruby, somewhat defeated by the realisation that Lucinda Marciano had been a complete wash-out in front of the critics and scouts, nodded solemnly in his direction and, with that, Calamity disappeared to catch his flight.

Blue and Serafina Marciano weren't far behind him, disgraced by what had unfolded. *What a disaster!*

17

A Star is Born

*P*ippa was in a whirl as she finally exited the stage into a throng of chattering girls. Molly and Maria pushed through the mass and launched themselves at her.

'Oh Pippa – you were breathtaking!' Molly cried, literally sobbing with joy.

'And what a song! Bloomin' marvellous!' echoed Maria, jumping up and down with excitement.

Pippa was unable to speak. It was more than she could have ever hoped for. She just wished her mum and Uncle Harry could have seen it – they'd have been so proud.

'We'd better get out of here quick – I've a feeling

this is going to get a bit ugly on the Lucifette front. Come and meet Mum and Dad, Pips . . . none of the Marciano clan will dare come near us so long as we're with Daddy. They're waiting for us to say goodbye in the car to avoid having to make any more small talk with Madame Ruby!'

The girls ran off up the path to where all the cars were waiting. It wasn't difficult to spot the Fitzfoster Bentley, together with the ever-obliging Eddie running around opening doors for their parents.

'Mummy . . . Daddy . . . what did you think?' Molly called.

Mrs Fitzfoster swung round, delighted to see her girls bounding towards her like puppies. 'Oh, girls. You were exquisite. Daddy and I are so proud of you. I think Madame Ruby was a little overwhelmed by the unexpected ending to the gala though. What a finale!'

'I know! Wasn't she amazing?' Molly said. 'Mum, Dad, this is Pippa Burrows.' The Fitzfosters turned their attention to the raven-haired beauty who sang like an angel.

'It's a pleasure to meet you finally, Pippa, darling. The twins have told us so much about you. And, my goodness, congratulations on your performance. What a voice!' As Mrs Fitzfoster swept Pippa up, Pippa

♥ 166 ♥

imagined she was in the arms of her own mother.

'Oh thank you soooo much. I'm so happy to meet you and Mr Fitzfoster. The girls never stop talking about you both.' Pippa was beaming with pride and admiration.

'Is that right?' Mr Fitzfoster asked. 'Well, perhaps you ought to come and stay with us at home in the Christmas holidays. I'm pretty sure you girls won't be able to last four whole weeks without seeing each other!'

'That's a wonderful idea, darling,' said Mrs Fitzfoster. 'I'll give your mother a call to fix it. Bye-bye, my darlings. I know it's the end of term and I've only to wait until tomorrow but I can't wait to have you home again. Eddie will be back to collect you at noon tomorrow – make sure you're all packed and ready. Have a lovely last night together. I'm sure you've tons to talk about.'

'Yes, and when you get home, you can tell us exactly what went on behind the scenes at tonight's show,' Mr Fitzfoster said. 'I'd bet my biggest diamond on the fact that you two twizzles were up to your necks in the plot to expose that little Marciano fraudster!' He winked at his girls, secretly proud of their high jinks. After all, how could he ever scold them – it wasn't their fault they'd inherited the infamous Fitzfoster mischief gene. He chuckled to himself as the old Bentley bounced away up the drive.

Molly, Maria and Pippa stood together in the night air as they had done that first evening of term when they'd met in their dorm, like three perfect corners that made up the triangle of friendship.

'What a night!' giggled Maria, hugging the girls in turn.

'Truly amazing!' Molly agreed.

Pippa was overcome with all the emotions of the day. From start to finish it had been a whirlwind, and now it was over, she found herself missing the adventure already.

'Don't cry, Pippa. There's plenty more fun where that came from – and just think, anyone who's anyone in showbiz got to hear your beautiful melody and lyrics tonight. You were a triumph!'

As Pippa opened her mouth to answer, Miss Hart's voice interrupted them from the path behind. 'Finally . . . there you are, girls,' she called out in relief. 'I honestly feel as though I've spent the entire evening tracking you Fitzfosters down – and as for you, Miss Burrows, there are definitely conversations to be had following today's most irregular events!'

Pippa winced and looked at Maria, but Maria, for once, had nothing to say. None of them had thought about how they'd explain Pippa's miraculous reappearance to Miss Hart!

'But all of that can wait for the moment,' Miss Hart continued, and as she stepped into the light on the gravel, the terrified trio saw that she was not alone. A tall, handsome man joined them.

'Pippa Burrows,' Miss Hart gestured to her companion. 'I would like you to meet your first *mega-fan*.' The man took Pippa's hand and shook it firmly.

'Great to meet you, Miss Burrows. I'm Emmett Fuller, Director of Universal Music,' he stated. The girls gasped in astonishment.

'I watched your performance this evening with keen interest and, with your permission, would very much like to follow your development here at L'Etoile, with a view to signing you to my record label in the future.'

'Oh my goodness . . .' Pippa stammered. 'M . . . M . . . Mr Fuller – I don't know what to say. Oh my goodness.'

Emmett Fuller grinned. He loved this bit of the job – seeing the hope twinkle in a young artist's eyes for the first time. 'Just say you're interested and that'll be it for the moment. We'll keep in touch via my dear friend Miss Hart here, who'll make sure I receive all your latest material.'

Helen Hart, who, if Molly wasn't mistaken, while nodding in agreement, also seemed to be gazing at Mr Fuller. Something's definitely going on there, she thought with glee. And what's more, the admiration seemed to be mutual. Emmett Fuller continued his conversation with Pippa, but all the while he barely took his eyes off Miss Hart.

'Thanks for everything Miss Hart, Mr Fuller,' Pippa said as she shook his hand.

'Yes, thank you!' Molly piped up. 'I'm Molly Fitzfoster, BTW. And this is my sister, Maria. We haven't been introduced. Great to meet you, Mr Fuller. Hope to again very soon. I sing too. Perhaps you'll come again to another performance?'

Maria smiled at her sister – ever graceful, but ever the opportunist for her own piece of the action.

The girls ran off back to Garland in silence, each saving their own explosion of excitement for the minute they were alone in their room. So much to discuss, and only one evening in which to do it before the Christmas holidays.

Two hours later, totally stuffed from the midnight feast to rival all midnight feasts, Maria, Molly and Pippa had exhausted every avenue of the day's events.

'Fancy Mr Fuller being there anyway!' Maria marvelled.

'If that's not fate, I don't know what is!' Molly exclaimed, attempting to brush a carpet of biscuit crumbs from her duvet.

'I know. Can't wait to hear the feedback from your performances too, though, girls. I overheard some great big American wearing massive spectacles praising "the fabulous diamond twins" as I left the theatre.'

'Are you kidding?! Big black-framed specs with ten-centimetre-thick lenses?' Pippa nodded, oblivious to the significance of what she'd just said.

'That's Calamity Mossback!' Molly exploded.

Pippa looked blank.

'THE Calamity Mossback! He's only the BIGGEST talent scout in Hollywood . . . and I don't just mean he's eaten too many doughnuts!'

Maria and Pippa collapsed into giggles. 'I can go to sleep a happy girl now,' Molly continued, stifling a yawn.

'Yes, let's all turn in, shall we?' agreed Maria. 'I don't think I can take much more excitement today. And we need to get up super-early to pack – we haven't done a thing tonight and Miss Coates'll be on the warpath first thing if she sees this mess. Looks like a bomb's gone off in a cake factory in here.'

''Night, sisters, well done on a great end to a great term. I've got enough material to keep the blog busy for the entire Christmas period! Roll on January's adventures!' Maria mused.

'I'm not sure I'll even be allowed back next term! Won't know until I've had a dressing down from Miss Hart tomorrow morning. I've got some real explaining to do – I'll be lucky not to be expelled for the stunt I've pulled today.'

'Don't worry, Pips – the Fuller Factor will smooth things over there . . . didn't you see the way they looked at each other? If he's as interested in you as he made out, it'll be in L'Etoile's interest to nurture every aspect of you – you know Madame Ruby'll never turn down an opportunity like that!' Maria grinned.

'And anyway – no matter how bad it is for you – just take comfort in the fact that Lucifette's probably been grounded for the rest of her life for embarrassing the Marcianos like that. Look, just tell Miss Hart the truth, the whole truth and nothing but the truth. She'll understand your succumbing to the temptation Lucifette laid at your feet. But for the record – 'scuse the pun – no more sneaking off for imaginary deals – got it? There aren't any shortcuts to success, just a whole lot of hard work, I'm afraid – but while we're working hard we can have some serious fun!'

Molly's eyes flashed with delight. ''Night, darlings, . . . 'night, lovelies . . . 'night, dudettes . . . 'night, starlets . . .'

'M O O O O O L L L L L L L L Y Y Y Y Y ! ! ! ! SHHHHHHHHHHHHH! And with that Maria launched a well-aimed slipper at her sister's head.

''Night, L'Etoilettes,' Molly whispered.

Would you like to go to L'Etoile too?

Turn the page for a reminder of who's who . . .

Alpha 1

Maria Fitzfoster	Pianist
Molly Fitzfoster	Singer/Actress
Pippa Burrows	Singer
Lydia Ambrose	Cellist/Double Bassist
Belle Brown	Ballet Dancer
Amanda Lloyd	Dancer
Daisy Mansfield	Bassoonist
Alice Parry	Singer/Actress
Sofia Vincenzi	Opera Singer/Actress
Lara Walters	Drummer/Percussionist

Beta 1

Nancy Althorpe	Actress
Elizabeth Jinks	Dancer
Charlotte Kissimee	Singer
Corine Sequoia	Singer/Actress
Heavenly Smith	Dancer
Faye Summers	Fashion Expert
Autumn Costello	Pianist
Betsy Harris	Pianist
Lucinda Marciano	Singer / Daughter of Blue & Serafina Marciano
Sally Sudbury	Actress / the Marcianos' Housekeeper's Daughter

Friends and Family ♥

Fitzfosters

The ever-obliging Eddie — The Fitzfoster Family Driver

Albie Good — The Fitzfoster Online Fashion Delivery Boy

Marcianos

Maggie Sudbury — Marciano Family Housekeeper

Elodie Wyatt — Mr Blue Marciano's Secretary

Burrows

Mrs Olivia Burrows — Pippa Burrows' Mother

Uncle Harry Burrows — Pippa Burrows' Uncle

♥ Talent Spotters and Staff ♥

Blue Marciano — Famous Hollywood Film Director

Serafina Marciano — Famous Hollywood Actress

Emmett Fuller — President, Universal Music Publishing

Calamity Mossback — Top Hollywood Talent Manager

L'Etoile Staff

Ruby Rose D'Arcy	Headmistress of L'Etoile
Miss Helen Hart	Deputy Headmistress of L'Etoile
Miss Sophie Bell	Housemistress of Monroe (Yellow)
Miss Mary Coates	Housemistress of Garland (Blue)
Lola Rose D'Arcy	Founder of L'Etoile
Mrs Rene Spittleforth	1 Alpha Form Tutor and Maths Teacher
Mr Victor McDoody	1 Beta Form Tutor and Science Master
Mrs Irene Mackle	Head Dinner Lady
Miss Natalia Seminova	Dance Teacher
Sister Patricia Payne	School Nurse
Mr Howard Potts	Music Maestro
Miss Emma Fleming	Drama Teacher
Mrs Audrey Butter	History Teacher

Second Term at L'Etoile
School for Stars

Can't wait to find out what happened
after the Christmas holidays?
Join Molly, Maria and Pips to find out . . .

1

L'Étoile, Sweet L'Étoile

'Molllly!' Maria shouted to her sister. 'Would you please shut that window – it's like an iceberg in here.'

Reluctantly, Molly tumbled backwards onto her bed, slamming the window shut as she fell.

'Where on earth can she be?' Molly groaned. 'I can't believe it's been nearly a whole month since we've seen our lovely Pippa. Barbados was amazebells and all that, but a bit last minute and I would far rather have had some fun at home with her.'

'Don't be so ungrateful, Moll,' Maria snapped. 'Do you know how many girls dream of having a holiday like the one we've just had?'

'I know, I know – I just miss her, that's all. Plus, I can't wait to give her her Christmas present.' Molly undid the bow on the little red box for about the tenth time since they'd arrived back at L'Etoile that morning, to admire the little gold star necklace engraved with a 'P'. 'She's going to absolutely love it!'

'I have to agree there, Moll. Mum really does have the best taste ever and the fact that all three of us have one, the same little L'Etoile star – each with our initial on – makes it all the more special.'

'I know! M, M and P. BFFs! It was such a shame Pips couldn't come and stay with us over Christmas, but like Mum said, hopefully this necklace will make up for us doing a disappearing act the for the whole break.'

'Yo! Anyone ho-ome?' came an excited voice from the corridor. All at once, the door burst open and Pippa appeared, loaded with bags and sporting her best attempt at a posh 'hair up' do to impress Miss Molly.

'Pips!' Molly shrieked, launching herself at Pippa, knocking her backwards into the corridor. 'And you've done your hair! Very sophisticated.'

'What a welcome,' Pippa giggled, delighted her

efforts hadn't gone unnoticed. 'Oh, girls. I've missed you so much! Can't wait to hear all your news.'

'What took you so long?' asked Molly. 'It's typical. I've been watching for you out of the window for the last hour – and then the second my back is turned, you show up!'

'It's like I told you, Molly – what is that saying about a watched pot never boiling?' said Maria with a grin.

Pippa and Molly both gave her their very best 'put-a-sock-in-it' look.

'So come on then, tell me . . . what's the goss?' Pippa asked, as she dragged her case onto the bed and started to unpack.

'I don't know where to begin,' Maria answered. 'Have you been keeping up with the Yours, L'Etoilette blog while we've been on hols?'

'Yes. I loved all your backstage blogs about the Christmas gala, but all of that was mainly school stuff – what's new with you two? I want to hear about all the latest Fitzfoster twin shenanigans since we said goodbye,' said Pippa.

'Ha! Ok. But first things first – is it present time, Mimi?' Molly asked Maria desperately.

'I can't believe you've waited this long!' Maria said

and then turned to Pippa. 'It's just a little something from Mum . . . erm . . . and us, to say happy Christmas and so sorry you couldn't come and stay with us. Mum felt so guilty for having to cancel our sleepover, she bought us all matching presents!'

Molly dragged Pippa over to sit on her bed and handed her the little red box with the bow, now frayed and untidy from too much tying and untying. 'Mum said it's so we can always feel close to one another, even when we are apart.'

Pippa was intrigued. 'Oh, but I haven't bought you girls anything. You shouldn't have . . .' Pippa was speechless when she saw the beautiful gold star necklace glittering up at her, with the letter 'P' inscribed in the centre. 'Oh my goodness, I love it!' she exclaimed. 'I don't think I've ever had anything so gorgeous! Thank you soooo much, girls. Quick, Molly, will you put it on for me?'

Molly was on cloud nine. In some ways getting the right gift for someone who loved it, was far more fun than receiving one.

'Look Pips – we all match now.' The twins held out their stars, both inscribed with the letter 'M', for her to see.

'I just don't know what to say. Really, thanks a

million, girls. This means the world to me,' Pippa said, clutching it tightly.

'And I have a little something for you too, Pips.' Maria said, handing over a silver DVD. 'I would have posted it to you over Christmas but didn't get a chance to download it before we went away.'

'What is it?' Pippa asked.

'It's a recording of your performance at the Christmas gala . . . so you can show your Mum and Uncle Harry. Maybe it'll go some way to make up for them not being there for your big moment.'

'You're kidding me! I can't believe it. Is there anything you girlies haven't thought of?' Pippa said, turning the disc over and over in her hands. She couldn't wait to show her family – and to watch it back herself. 'Ooooh I love you girls! What a welcome!'

'Right, now it's my turn,' she said, rummaging around in her music bag.

'What have you lost?' Molly asked, excitedly.

'Ah ha! Here it is. Actually this can be my Christmas present to you two,' Pippa said, sliding a CD into the player. 'While you were sunning yourselves in the Caribbean, I spent pretty much every day of the holidays in the studio with Uncle Harry, working on some new songs. And here's one I wrote for you both.

It's called "Friends Forever".' She pressed play and the song burst out of the speakers.

Ooooh . . . just little old me,
Oooh . . . then we were three.

I can't explain the feeling,
The one that leaves me reeling.

I never thought that friends could be
A second kind of family,

Ooooh . . . this ain't no short-term endeavour
Oooooh . . . you know we're friends forever . . .

The L'Etoilette trio sat bobbing their heads to the beat, grinning from ear to ear as the track continued to play.

'It's BRILLIANT!' exclaimed Maria and Molly, in unison as it finished.

'I just don't know how you do it. And I love the lyrics . . .' Molly began singing at the top of her voice:

Ooooh . . . just little old me,
Ooooh . . . then we were three.

'Well, if you've picked it up that quickly – at least we know it's catchy,' Pippa beamed, loving the twin's response to all her hard work.

Knock, knock.

'Who is it?' Maria called out.

A voice boomed through the door, making them jump. 'L'ETOILETTES, WOULD YOU PLEASE KEEP THE NOISE DOWN!'

Who on earth was that? All of a sudden, Sally Sudbury thrust open the bedroom door, which hit the wall with a crash.

'SALLY!' Molly cried with delight. 'Sally, Sally – so good to see you. You look great. I love your boots – so this season! How are you?'

'Really, Molly? Thanks!' Sally said as she hugged the girls, delighted her Christmas-present footwear was a hit with the queen of fashion. 'I'm good, thanks . . . really good, as a matter of fact. Guess what?' she almost burst with excitement, 'Lucifette's not coming back to L'Etoile this term!'

'WHAT?' Maria, Molly and Pippa gasped with glee.

'Now that is what I call a Christmas present!' Maria joked.

'Oh Sally – that's wonderful news. Quick – grab a fairy cake,' Molly pointed to a box of half-eaten homemade cakes on the bed. 'And tell us everything!'

Sally sat down and took a deep breath. 'You should have seen her after the gala. Boy, was I ever in the wrong place at the wrong time. Stupidly, I stayed backstage after I'd done my poem because I wanted to witness her get busted – but I didn't think far enough ahead to realise I would be the first person she'd run into as she came off stage! Honestly, she was in that much of a rage, I thought she was going to knock me out!'

'Oh, Sally, you poor thing. But by the way, your poem was simply wonderful. I didn't get a chance to say after the show. You're so clever,' Pippa said, and then realised she was changing the subject too soon. 'Sorry – do carry on – then what happened?'

'Oh, thanks so much! I'd quite forgotten that went so well with everything that's happened since,' Sally said. 'Anyway, as you can imagine, she was furious and mortified about being caught out like that in front of everyone. She was ranting and raving at such a pitch all the way to the car, I couldn't even understand what she was saying. I thought she was going to bust a vocal chord!'

'Hoped she would, you mean,' chuckled Maria.

'No such luck. It wasn't a pretty sight. As you know we didn't even go back to the dorm to get our bags. Miss Coates had to pack them and give them to the courier the next day. Mr and Mrs Marciano wouldn't hear of us going back to Garland. They couldn't bear the humiliation of having to see anyone after the show – for Lucifette – or themselves! So we were whisked straight off to London. From what I gather, the Marcianos sent a fairly large cheque for the L'Etoile Founder's Fund – to try and smooth over the embarrassment.'

'Well, they do say money talks,' said Pippa.

'Yes and Lucifette's walked!' said Maria, excitedly. 'So, is she gone for good, Sal? And, more to the point, how did you manage to get them to let you come back to L'Etoile by yourself? I should have thought Lucifette would have needed to bully you more than ever after what happened.'

'Well, that's the funniest part!' Sally said. 'That family is so arrogant, Mrs Marciano actually said as part of my punishment – for not somehow preventing the situation – I was to come back to L'Etoile on my own rather than having the honour of being by her daughter's side!'

'How lucky is that!? You're going to have the time of your life this term, Sally. You'll feel free for the first time in years I should think,' Molly said. 'And judging by the fact you're still breathing, I'm guessing they don't know you helped expose Lucifette then?'

'Oh, don't. In actual fact, for a minute I thought she might have realised that I was the only other person who knew the whole story to betray her. But luckily she thinks I'm too stupid to think for myself. She's put the whole thing down to Pippa chickening out of the fake Universal Music audition.'

'Oh, great!' said Pippa. 'So I am public enemy numero uno. Just tell me she's not coming back – ever!'

'Sadly, we're not that lucky. She managed to talk the Marcianos into letting her spend a term at a special acting school in LA. She's aiming to be back next term so she can sit the end-of-year exams and pass with flying colours.'

'Well, that's something to look forward to then,' said Maria sarcastically.

'What? Lucifette coming back – or end-of-year exams?' groaned Molly. Just listen to us!' she continued. 'Let's focus on the positives and be happy for now that we've got a whole term without her. Think how deliciously uneventful it's going to be.'

But as we know, Story-seeker, those are famous last words. Life is never quite what you expect it to be!

the orion star

Sign up for **the orion star**
newsletter to get inside information
about your favourite children's authors
as well as exclusive competitions and
early reading copy giveaways.

www.orionbooks.co.uk/newsletters